Kondo wa zettai ni jama shimasen! Novel 2
by Soratani Reina, Harukawa Haru
© 2020 SORATANI REINA, HARUKAWA HARU/
GENTOSHA COMICS INC.
All rights reserved.
Original Japanese edition published in 2020 by
GENTOSHA COMICS Inc.
English translation rights arranged worldwide with
GENTOSHA COMICS Inc. through Digital Catapult Inc., Tokyo.

Seven Seas press and purchase enquiries can be sent to
Marketing Manager Lianne Sentar at press@gomanga.com.
Information regarding the distribution and purchase of
digital editions is available from Digital Manager CK Russell
at digital@gomanga.com.

Follow Seven Seas Entertainment online at
sevenseasentertainment.com.

TRANSLATION: Kimberly Chan
ADAPTATION: T. Anne
COVER DESIGN: H. Qi
LOGO DESIGN: George Panella
INTERIOR DESIGN: Clay Gardner
INTERIOR LAYOUT: Jennifer Elgabrowny
PROOFREADER: Jade Gardner
COPY EDITOR: Meg van Huygen
LIGHT NOVEL EDITOR: Katy M. Kelly
PREPRESS TECHNICIAN: Melanie Ujimori, Jules Valera
PRODUCTION MANAGER: Lissa Pattillo
EDITOR-IN-CHIEF: Julie Davis
ASSOCIATE PUBLISHER: Adam Arnold
PUBLISHER: Jason DeAngelis

ISBN: 978-1-64827-339-1
Printed in Canada
First Printing: November 2022
10 9 8 7 6 5 4 3 2 1

I Swear I Won't Bother You AGAIN!

NOVEL 2

WRITTEN BY
Reina Soratani

ILLUSTRATED BY
Haru Harukawa

Airship

Seven Seas Entertainment

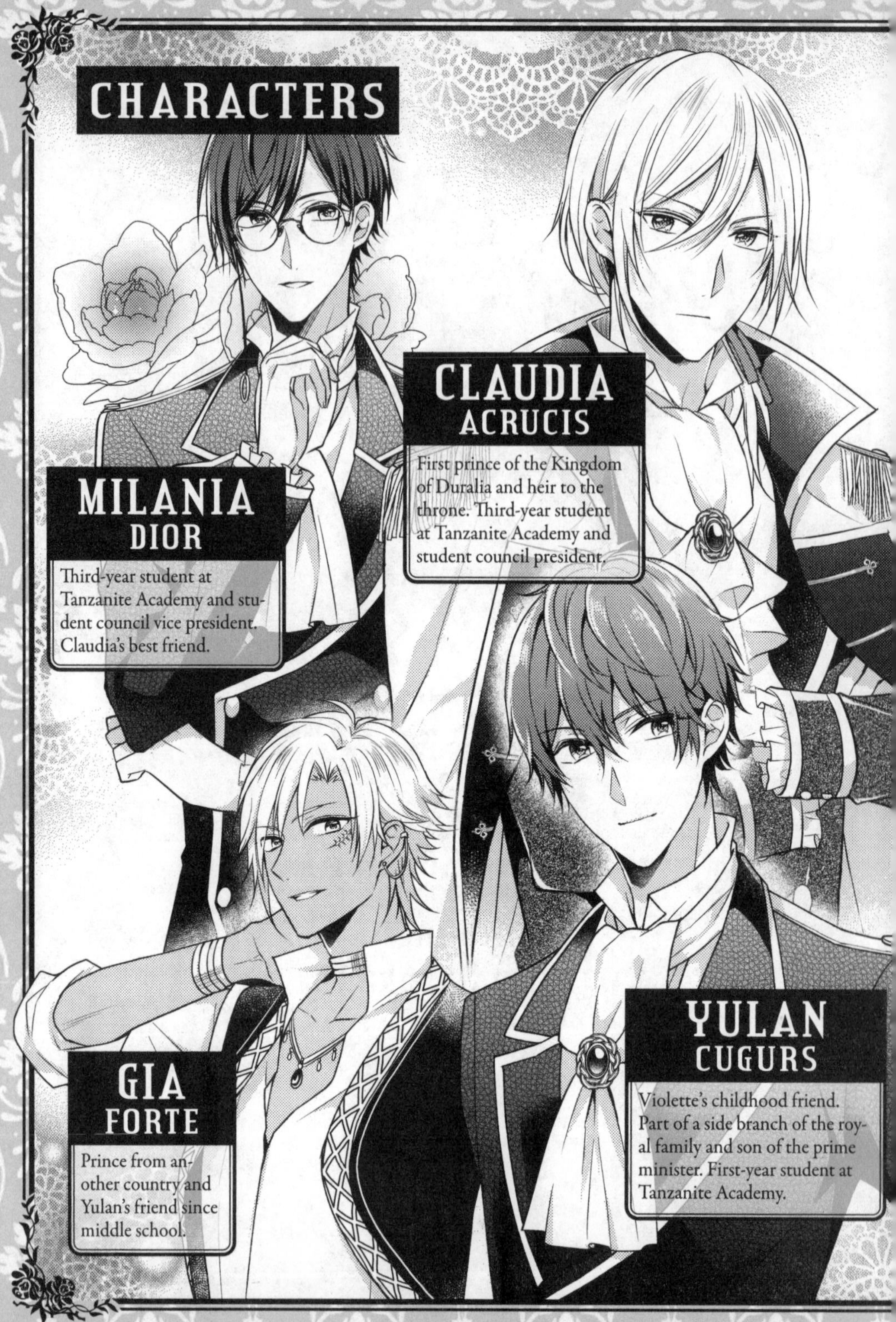
CHARACTERS
CLAUDIA ACRUCIS
First prince of the Kingdom of Duralia and heir to the throne. Third-year student at Tanzanite Academy and student council president.
MILANIA DIOR
Third-year student at Tanzanite Academy and student council vice president. Claudia's best friend.
YULAN CUGURS
Violette's childhood friend. Part of a side branch of the royal family and son of the prime minister. First-year student at Tanzanite Academy.
GIA FORTE
Prince from another country and Yulan's friend since middle school.

MARYJUNE VAHAN

Second daughter of Duke Vahan. Violette's half sister and first-year student at Tanzanite Academy.

MARIN

The maid who serves Violette.

VIOLETTE REM VAHAN

Eldest daughter of Duke Vahan, imprisoned for the attempted murder of her half sister. Sent back in time. Second-year student at Tanzanite Academy.

ROSETTE MEGAN

Princess of the neighboring country of Lithos and second-year student at Tanzanite Academy.

⇾Table of Contents⇽

48 Before the Tipping Point

THANKS TO MARYJUNE'S SLIGHT change of heart, Violette felt a little less gloomy. While Maryjune's way of thinking hadn't flipped completely, she'd come to terms with the fact that they needed to keep up appearances. That was the most important thing.

However, this still wouldn't be enough to change Violette's life. Violette would continue to be excluded from the family circle, dragged out and yanked back in as they saw fit. She considered steeling her heart and abandoning the idea of getting closer to Maryjune.

Although Violette knew where she wanted to be after graduation, she was stuck for now. In fact, if someone were to notice her half-hearted attempts, that would seal off her route to the nunnery. It wasn't unheard of for a duke's daughter to seek sisterhood of her own volition, but it would certainly raise some questions. Her father especially would have some choice words for her, and he'd marry her off for the sake of the Vahan name.

In truth, Violette found that path much more plausible than actually becoming a nun.

Would that kind of life be peaceful in its own way? she wondered.

If Maryjune changed her attitude, she'd attract less vitriol from others. There would always be people who hunted for flaws, seeing cherry dimples as ugly pockmarks, but their inflated malice made them easy to pick out. Thus, Violette decided to focus only on averting the worst possible outcomes at the academy. She didn't care if people hated Maryjune; her only concern was how Maryjune reacted to them.

"...Hello? Vio, can you hear me?" came Yulan's voice.

"Oh! Err, sorry. What is it?" Violette responded.

"Is this right?"

"Um... Yes, it's fine."

The school library was so enormous it could house all the students at once. Plenty of other rooms in the academy—many of which were deemed salons—functioned as libraries, but only this one truly embodied the concept. It had the largest collection of books available, not to mention an abundance of seating. It was like the main office to all the smaller branch offices.

Today, crowds of students were gathered in both the salons and the library. There was only one reason these pupils would willingly choose to stay after school to study in the library, their textbooks, notes, and writing instruments spread out around them.

"I'm sure you know the answer even if I don't check your work," Violette said.

With a grin, her friend replied, "Yeah, but I thought you might praise me if I got it right. Hee hee."

Yulan was in such good spirits that one wouldn't have imagined he was in the middle of studying. He didn't even particularly *enjoy* studying, despite his knack for it. No, the fact that he was elated almost to the point of humming was simply because Violette was at his side. He wasn't even focused on studying at all, but it was a necessary evil, so Violette figured she would kill two birds with one stone by helping him.

"Let's see... How about I give you a reward if you answer everything correctly?"

"Really?! All right!"

The two of them were studying as equals, meaning there was no real reason for Violette to play the part of his teacher. Still, she had no problem treating him to food somewhere if Yulan wanted it. And with his smarts, Yulan was guaranteed to get all the questions right.

"Then you'd best finish before closing time," Violette told him.

"'Kaaay."

At that moment, his lackadaisical expression turned serious. Though he was no longer smiling, Yulan still radiated calm. While his droopy eyes weren't as sharp as Violette's, they had a real softness to them—although the way he looked at his notes wasn't particularly gentle.

Indeed, exams were approaching for the two of them. The school year was divided into trimesters, and each had two exams for a total of six per year. They lasted three days, testing students' academic abilities across all subjects, so they were naturally de-tested. The upcoming exam wouldn't be so bad, since it was the first of the new school year, but the questions were cumulative; as the year went on, the tests would become more and more difficult.

Brute force cramming would be impossible. If they absorbed all the material as they learned it in class, studying would be unnecessary, but that was impossible too. Thus, the students utilized a small loophole: upperclassmen passing down their exams to their juniors. It wasn't nefarious in the way cheating was but rather a trivial strategy to help students to pass.

"I'm glad you held on to your old exams," Yulan said to Violette.

"There's no way I would throw them out. I knew you would need them."

Teachers had very little free time. Revising those six annual exams every time would've been far too much work. More importantly, as the contents of the lessons weren't changed, altering the exam questions alone would've created a lot of extra work. Therefore, each exam rarely changed across the years. Even if they weren't exact replicas, roughly 60 percent, maybe even 70 percent of the questions remained the same. The only real differences were in the phrasing or the numbers; the methods were unchanged.

Only the end-of-year exam for students advancing to the next grade was completely revised each time, negating this strategy. Still, it was only a way to make things easier, not a surefire way to succeed.

"Still, I thought you might keep them for...y'know."

Violette had helped Yulan with his exams back in middle

school, but he'd assumed she would bestow her blessing else-where. Considering he already had a strong grasp on the material, he thought she would feel obligated to help her younger sister, Maryjune. The girl hardly seemed to know left from right when it came to school.

Reading the apprehension in his gaze, Violette said curtly, "I don't intend to push her if she doesn't ask. Besides, I think she'll be fine." She glanced back down at her textbook.

Surely Violette had a better grasp of Maryjune's intellect than the girl herself. In the past, Violette had despised her, so she'd planned on sabotaging Maryjune rather than aiding her. Yet Maryjune had still shone brightly as the top student. This time around, Violette thought of offering to help the girl if she asked, but it didn't seem like there would be an opportunity to do so. Maryjune didn't know what it was like to struggle with her studies—she was a genius.

"Let's drop it for now and focus on *your* studying. If you don't get good grades, it'll defeat the point of me helping you, right?"

"Yeah, I'll do my best."

"I'm glad to hear it."

Once he said that, she could assume that Yulan would do well. He wasn't the sort who'd get test anxiety either. No, the one who really had to double down on their studies was Violette.

"This one might be a bit tough," Yulan muttered as he resumed focus, his voice quiet enough that no one could hear.

Violette was taking this exam for the second time, but that didn't necessarily make it any easier. Even though she'd studied hard last time, her grades had been overshadowed by Maryjune's amazing performance. Her father had rattled off all sorts of complaints as a result.

While Violette wasn't a genius, she was much smarter than average. And she'd scored fairly well the last time she took the exam, so she had ended up arguing with her father. This time, she would listen quietly in the hopes that he would quickly move on to praising Maryjune instead. To that end, she had to achieve grades that were just good enough. However, she had never imagined that she would be taking this test again, and the memory of their fight dampened her spirits.

The biggest obstacle was that she had no one she could borrow an old exam from. She was acquainted with some upperclassmen, sure, but that was all they were: acquaintances. None of them would explain things to her, nor was she the type to request it. Therefore, the studying strategy most other students used was out of the question for her.

Since she wouldn't be able to predict what might be on the exam, she instead had to cram every detail from the textbooks into her head. If only her memory was good enough to recall the exam questions from a year before her imprisonment... Well, if she could manage that, she could have just memorized all the material in class to begin with.

Violette found even the first exam of the year arduous, so when each subsequent exam proved even worse than the last, she found herself fantasizing about burning down the academy. The process had absolutely fried her brain.

Thinking back on it now, she winced at the immensity of the hurdle before her. While neither sister could review old exams, her father would no doubt demand to know why Violette hadn't reached the top of her class even though Maryjune had. Only the numbers mattered; her efforts meant nothing to him. No matter how hard she toiled, he would see Violette as inferior, lazier, and more irresponsible than Maryjune.

If everyone had an innate talent, then some things could surely only be learned through hard work. Regardless, Violette's efforts were no match for Maryjune's genius. For that, her father scorned her.

I believe he scolded me for "making excuses."

He'd told her not to use talent as an excuse. The same lips that extolled Maryjune as a prodigy had reprimanded Violette for her perceived indolence. It had dawned on Violette then how biased this man was. She was on the receiving end of his prejudice countless times, eventually growing accustomed to the treatment, but back then, she had been tormented by his words. It had been roughly a year since then, so her memories of it now were somewhat fuzzy.

Violette knew that Maryjune was a genius, and she had long been aware that what she considered "effort" could never match up to that. That was why she was no longer pessimistic toward her lack of talent.

"Well, the results will speak for themselves," Violette said to herself.

It didn't matter how much she asserted that she did her best. It wouldn't overturn the fact that Maryjune eclipsed her. In the end, she had no choice but to plug away at her studies in a terribly inefficient way, just like her past self.

Without intending to, she let out a long, deep sigh.

Normally, no one would have noticed. However, the boy by her side prioritized her above everything else in the world. Even if he was immersed in his studies, there was no way Yulan would let Violette's little slip of gloom escape his ears.

49 Awareness and Priority

ALL AROUND VIOLETTE were the sounds of rustling fabric, nervous breaths, and pen tips scratching on paper. Even though the sounds were all faint, her nerves were stretched nearly to breaking, so they'd been grating on her ears for some time now. Her heart was thrumming so loudly in her ears that she worried others could hear it. No one could, of course.

"Vio, your hand stopped. Are you stuck?" Yulan asked.

"Huh? Oh, no, I'm fine."

Nope. No problems here. Rather, she was feeling pretty good about things. In fact, she thought she'd be able to get an even better score this time.

He nodded and flashed his signature grin. "Gotcha." He always took her words to heart.

While she wasn't having an issue with the material, she had a much *bigger* problem. Things were not, in fact, fine. She wondered if Yulan was too dense to realize it, but she believed in him, so she figured this problem of theirs would soon disappear. It had to do with the people they were with.

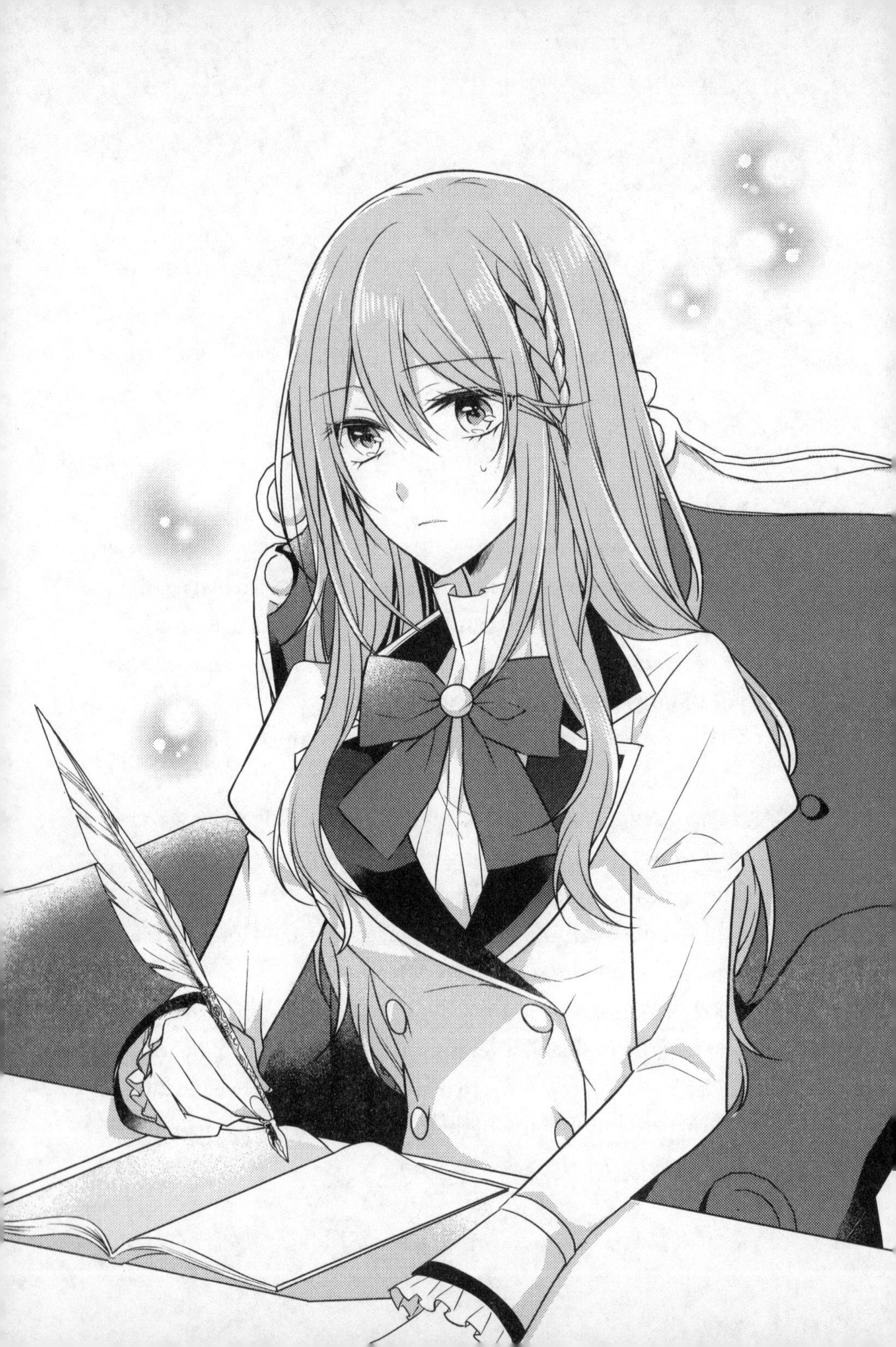

"Oh, Violette, that line will probably change," came a familiar voice. "I believe the teacher in charge has..."

Golden hair dangled in front of her. The owner's finger pointed to the sheet Violette was currently tackling. More specifically, it was a sheet from last year's exam.

Violette fully understood the situation she was in. Even so, she desperately wanted to ask: *How did things turn out like this?*

❧

It began when Yulan invited Violette to study for their exams. She felt no suspicion that anything was awry then—it was only natural that they'd study together, considering she was lending him her old exam. Violette didn't need the test anymore, so she tried to simply give it to him for good, but Yulan was so stubborn that they ended up shoving the documents back and forth between them. Those measly sheets of paper would only lie there unused at school otherwise; Violette worried that he wouldn't have them at hand when he reviewed at home.

It ultimately turned out to be no problem, since Yulan only intended to study with Violette. As such, they had gone to the library for several days.

Today, Violette looked for some empty seats like usual, but Yulan had other ideas.

He told her, "I got a third-year to bring last year's exam with him, so we'll study over there."

"What?"

It took her what felt like ages to process what he'd said. He beamed at her all the while, and although he didn't push her, he also didn't bother to explain. Instead, he stood there like a loyal dog, waiting for her to speak. Realizing he wasn't going to elaborate, Violette heaved a sigh that was both astonished and resigned.

"You know some third years, I see."

Violette knew he had acquaintances, but she couldn't imagine Yulan being close with any of them. He was always mild-mannered with her, but she knew the face he showed her couldn't be all there was to him.

Violette knew that Yulan didn't get along with Claudia. In fact, the entire academy had picked up on the complicated relationship between the two. By extension, Yulan would likely want to avoid Claudia's classmates—that is, the other third-year students. At least, that was what she'd believed up until now. Apparently, she was wrong.

When she thought about it, she realized it wasn't all that strange for someone with his personality to socialize with others outside his own grade.

"I guess you could say that."

His cryptic response puzzled her.

"C'mon, Vio. I think he's already here."

"Right. Wouldn't want to keep him waiting."

Yulan's expression darkened for a moment, but he immediately recovered. It was such a subtle change that anyone else would have overlooked it, but she was close enough to him to have seen it. She knew that if she pressed him for answers, he wouldn't budge. Once they met the person in question, all would be revealed, so there was no need to fret.

But along the way, Violette began to realize where they were headed. Her vague guess solidified into belief, and she glanced at Yulan in shock several times over. He didn't say a word. She was walking nearly beside him, lagging just a little behind, so he should've been able to sense her feelings. In other words, he knew and purposely wasn't giving her an explanation. Eventually, they came to a stop.

They had arrived at the student council room.

Now the two of them were in the student council president's salon, and Claudia, the last person Violette had expected to see, was looking over her studies.

Really, how had things turned out this way?

I Swear I Won't Bother You AGAIN!

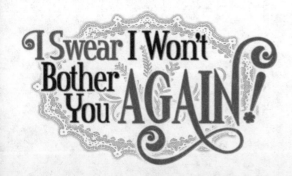

50 | One Standard

STUDYING WITH VIOLETTE, sitting side by side while engaging in light banter, was absolute bliss for Yulan.

The guidance given without any hesitation. Her gaze brushing graciously across the paper. Her gesture of placing the tip of the pen on her lips. The wrinkles in her brow and slightly puffed-out cheeks that changed into a beaming smile whenever a problem was solved. Resolute beauty. The innocence of a child challenging a puzzle.

Observing each of Violette's expressions while he studied was like toiling away with soothing music in the background. If study sessions were this enjoyable, he would do this not only during exams but every single day. That way, he could always get full marks.

However, it seemed a little too one-sided. He was troubled by the fact that he had nothing to offer her.

"Hey, Vio."

"Hm? Having some trouble?"

"Yeah, could you please explain this part?"

"There's a trick to it. If you read the problem carefully, you'll find the answer."

He pointed to a suitable problem, drawing Violette's attention. He memorized every single word that fell from her lips, locking away what he really wanted to say deep in his heart.

Vio, you don't have anyone to teach you, right?

Yulan knew the answer without needing to ask. Violette didn't have many acquaintances among the third-year students, and he couldn't imagine any of them would let her peek at their past exams. Still, he hated the thought of her studying side by side with anyone else.

Never before had he so deeply regretted being a year younger than her. At times, he did relish being her junior, but right now, he was green with envy. Ultimately, he just wanted to be in a position that benefited Violette. She could help him with his studies because he was a first-year student, but he couldn't teach her anything. Nevertheless, just thinking about it wouldn't fix things.

While he knew that their current arrangement was for Violette's sake, he couldn't help but feel useless and jealous as he watched.

⚜

"Whatcha worried 'bout?" Gia asked.

"Shut up," Yulan said flatly.

"You're scary when you ain't puttin' a face on." Gia could guess what was bugging Yulan from the tone of his voice and the revulsion in his eyes.

"If Miss Vio sees you like that, you'll scare her," he said.

"I wouldn't do something so foolish."

"Ah, I guess you're right."

It was break time, and there were still some people left inside the classroom. Either Yulan didn't care if there were onlookers, or he didn't think it was an issue because of his usual persona. Gia figured it was the latter. Those who knew the usual Yulan would probably be surprised if they saw him like this, but they'd likely interpret it positively, like it was a charming contrast from his usual manner. Yulan was just that popular.

"So what's troublin' you? Did somethin' happen to Princess?"

"I thought you stopped calling her that."

"Look, I told you that the moment I call her 'Miss Vio,' you let off this, like, dark aura. If she ain't here, I'll stick to what I usually do."

"Hmm. Okay."

Yulan had no idea that his gaze turned deadly sharp whenever Gia used Violette's nickname. If Gia was going to switch, Yulan wasn't about to stop him. While he didn't approve of the nickname "Princess," it didn't bother him as much as someone else using his own personal nickname for her. Gia thought his friend had tunnel vision, but Yulan had always reserved his kindness for Violette and Violette alone, so Gia decided not to press the issue. There would've been no point to it.

"Gia, you..." Yulan trailed off, then shifted from question to statement. "You don't know any third-years."

"At least ask me, man. You're right, though. I don't."

"If I don't know any, it's a given that you wouldn't."

"True."

Yulan's statement was quite blunt, and Gia was suspiciously quick to agree to the insult. There was such a thing as being too accepting of others' opinions...although truth be told, Gia likely had no interest in discussing it further. It was true, after all.

Gia became cordial acquaintances with his classmates and the other first-year students rather quickly whenever he interacted with them, but the way he looked made him stand out. Yulan's circumstances were similarly complex, though his couldn't be seen on the surface.

"Hey, ain't there a handful of people you fooled with your nice-guy act?"

"I didn't deceive anyone," Yulan retorted. "They just misunderstood me."

"That's what folks mean when they say, 'It's not what you say but how you say it.'"

"You're supposed to speak diplomatically to make a good first impression, no?"

"Wish it was as simple as that..."

Gia felt slightly troubled. Trying to convince someone who clearly had no intention of changing was just a waste of energy. They'd digressed far enough, he had to steer things back to the main topic.

"Somethin' up with the third years?" Gia asked.

"Exams are just around the corner."

"Come *on*, dude. Would it kill you to spell it out a bit more?"

Even Gia knew that they'd all be taking exams soon. While

he appeared to have a lax air and lifestyle, he maintained the bare minimum grades a prince should have...more or less. The question was how the exams and Yulan's search for third-year students were connected.

Gia's confused look earned him a glare from Yulan that said, *Are you stupid?* Thankfully, not many people would recognize it for what it was.

With a heavy sigh, Yulan explained, "I'm looking for someone who can lend Vio their old exams, but I'm not having any luck."

Originally, Violette had been the only person close to Yulan. Whenever possible, he showered her with love and affection. He wasn't the type to bother acting friendly around anyone with whom he barely interacted.

Gia and Yulan were famous in different ways, but Violette had notoriety that made people keep their distance. Yulan assessed everyone around him based on whether they would benefit or harm her and treated them accordingly. In other words, all the upperclassmen Yulan considered acquaintances were *also* people who felt something toward Violette. There was no way Yulan would choose to allow such uncertain factors near his precious treasure. But that meant that anyone he could use—or rather, depend on—was out of the equation.

"Guess I've got no other choice," Yulan muttered. Discomfort and resignation were written on his features.

"Hm?"

"It's nothing."

Gia's brow furrowed. He'd known Yulan long enough to have learned that hounding him further was a wasted effort. Anyway, he reassured himself, Yulan wasn't typically the sort to lash out at others for something he'd decided by himself. Even if this was a rare exception where he might, it should all work out as long as he was left alone.

In the end, Gia didn't have a clue what Yulan was thinking. What he *did* know was that Violette was bound to be confused for quite some time at tomorrow's study session.

51 Only if You Ask

IT TOOK VIOLETTE a long time to process what was happening. Everything had transpired in a flash, and she still wasn't quite sure what to do. She could feel herself being swept up in the tide. Not that it bothered her, necessarily, but she was worried about Yulan. She didn't want him to put up with all this for her sake.

As she worked away at the exam questions, she peeked at him from the corner of her eye. His expression was the same as always, and he was diligently solving the problems from her past exam. This had been his decision, so even if it *was* for her, she shouldn't intervene.

Maybe I'm worrying too much.

She chided herself for being so overprotective. Yulan was no longer the small, cute boy he had once been—he'd matured into a tall and reliable man. It would be rude for her to treat him like a child now.

In reality, Yulan was far more overprotective than she was, but he was a wolf in sheep's clothing; he'd never slip up and reveal what lay beneath his mask.

"You've got that one wrong, Violette." Claudia's voice wrested her from her thoughts.

"Huh?! Oh, um, where?" she asked in a tizzy.

"Look here. The example's a bit hard to understand, so it can confuse things."

"You're right."

"The teacher for that class does this a lot. I'm sure it'll show up on this year's exam too, so be prepared."

"Got it. Thank you."

Surprisingly, Claudia's teaching methods were easy to understand. It wasn't just his way of solving problems; he really got into the nitty-gritty of things like the teachers' habits. He often acted passively around Yulan because of the tension between them, but now Violette was reminded of what a talented person he was underneath. What caught her off guard most was how kind, careful, and thorough he was as he tutored her. Compared to before, the air between the two of them had softened quite a bit, but Violette knew that this didn't equal trust or forgiveness. They were locked in a dance where neither could decide if they should back away or try to come closer.

Claudia had agreed to help, so he was seeing it through with due diligence. Given his personality, Violette would've expected him to be more businesslike about it, but the atmosphere as they worked was quite peaceful. He continued to surprise her, and that perplexed her most of all.

"Are you all right, Vio?" Yulan asked. "Feeling tired?"

"Hm?"

"Let's take a short break," Milania suggested.

Milania closed the book in his hand with a loud *whump*. He and Claudia exchanged glances, nodding as they came to some sort of silent agreement. Picking up a stack of books, Milania stood and placed a hand not on Claudia's shoulder but Yulan's. In contrast to Yulan's suspicious expression, Milania's smile didn't crack. Whatever his emotions, they were locked tight behind it.

"Yulan, can you give me a hand for a bit?" Milania asked.

"Huh?" Yulan said.

"I was thinking about buying something on my way back from the library. I can't exactly have Mademoiselle Violette carry anything, nor can I leave you two alone in this room."

As the salon was owned by the student council, it couldn't be used unless a member was present. Brief restroom breaks were permitted, of course, but that tolerance didn't extend to a trip to the library and a detour on the way back. If he couldn't ask Violette, who was a lady, and Claudia, the other member, that left only Yulan.

"Besides, you'd know her tastes much better than I would, right?"

Yulan said nothing. He glared daggers at Milania but quickly donned his composed smile as he simmered with regret. Milania simply stood there waiting patiently, his posture unyielding. Claudia felt his own composure slipping; Yulan's ferocity rattled him even when it was directed at someone else. The turbulent air around them grew heavy—until an elegant voice rang out to break up the brewing storm.

"You should go with him, Yulan," Violette said.

"But, Vio…"

"It'll be good to get a breath of fresh air."

"Okay, I understand."

Just like that, it was as if the tension had never existed. The furrow in Yulan's brow that Milania had seen might as well have been an illusion. It was almost like he had two separate personalities.

"Shall we?" Milania pressed.

"Yeah." Yulan turned to the other two and said, "Make sure you take a break too."

"We know," replied Claudia.

"See you soon," said Violette.

The instant Yulan disappeared from Violette's line of sight behind the salon door, all the emotions on his face slid off and disappeared.

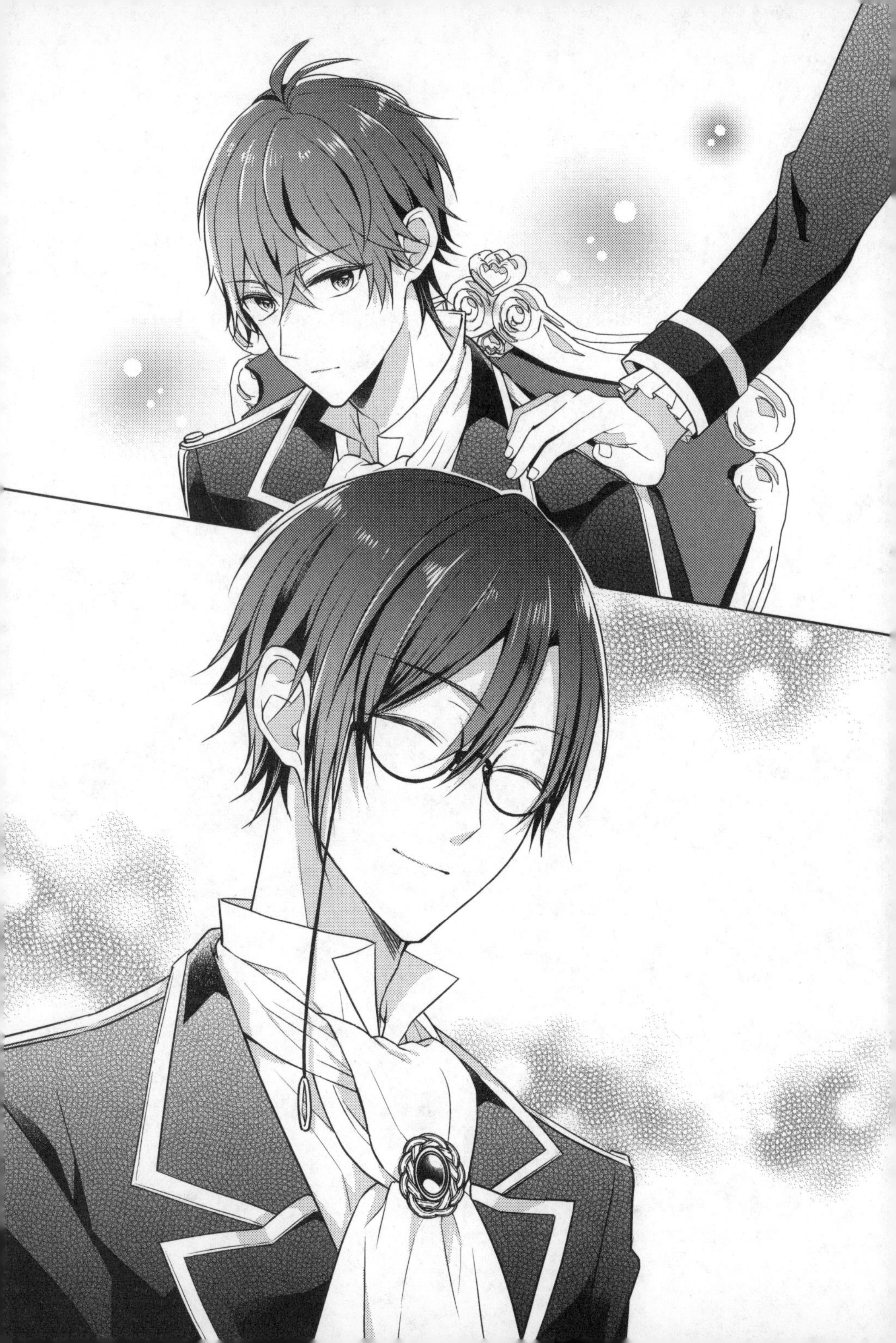

I Swear I Won't Bother You AGAIN!

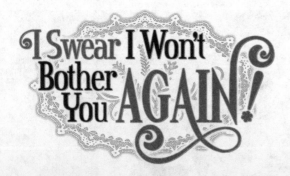

52 Tipping the Scales

YULAN WAS AN AMICABLE YOUNG MAN with a kind and gentle nature and a soft smile, or so most people believed. Yulan kept up appearances well enough that even Milania, who knew the true Yulan, occasionally fell for it. If Milania hadn't been Claudia's best friend, he certainly wouldn't know about Yulan's dual nature.

Currently, Yulan was boring into him with a gaze devoid of any emotion; it appeared his agitation had reached its zenith. Milania recalled Yulan maintaining his facade a bit more with him in the past, although that was primarily back in middle school.

"You've become rather sloppy lately," he told Yulan.

"Who, me? Could you just drop it and hurry up, please?"

"You don't act sweet and innocent around me anymore."

Miliana understood why Yulan was so cruel to Claudia, but as it was between the two of them, he didn't condemn him for it.

The relationship between Yulan and Claudia was well known, so most people were aware that things were awkward between the two of them. But Yulan wasn't foolish enough to let those around him suspect how intensely he loathed Claudia. The few people close to Claudia, like Milania and Gia, wouldn't give him trouble whether they knew or not—they'd had opportunities to get in the middle or spread rumors, and hadn't. So most people had no idea that Yulan and Claudia were separated by a ditch as deep as the abyss.

"Will it help Vio if I act friendly with you?" Yulan asked.

He wasn't frustrated by Milania's remarks; rather, he was brimming with contempt, like he was looking down at vermin. His gaze was ice-cold, striking enough to send a chill down anyone's spine.

Milania managed a wry smile. "You're always like this when Mademoiselle Violette is involved."

Normally, people looked out for themselves first, but Yulan had always prioritized Violette. This trait of his hadn't changed ever since Milania had first met the boy. If Yulan had to sacrifice his own self-worth to potentially aid her in some way, he would do it every time.

Just saying Violette's name had apparently struck a nerve; Yulan's grim expression intensified. If this was how he reacted when she was mentioned, Milania shuddered to think what would happen to those who insulted her. Surely he'd grind their bones into dust. Only if the words escaped Violette's ears would Yulan let them off the hook.

"If you're just going to keep blabbering, I'll head back first. I only went along with this because Vio told me to. It's not my job to keep you company," Yulan asserted. The openness felt rather liberating.

This reconfirmed how precious Violette was to Yulan, and that was exactly why Milania had doubts.

"I'm surprised you let Claudia get close to someone you hold so dear. I thought you didn't have a speck of trust in him, let alone goodwill."

Milania chose his words carefully, but he was essentially saying that Yulan should have nothing but disdain for Claudia, so deep and dark that it exceeded hatred. He wondered what turn of events had led Yulan to allow such a person near the apple of his eye. Bringing the person he treasured near the person he despised could only have been motivated by Yulan's love for Violette.

"That's irrelevant," Yulan replied. "Helping Vio with her troubles is more important than my feelings."

It was hardly an explanation, but it was clear he was once again putting her before himself. If he were to put her on a scale, Violette would outweigh everything in the world. His feelings toward Claudia were both complex and mysterious, but Yulan perceived him in the same manner he would any other lowlife next to his beloved.

"She needed a way to study for her exams, so I judged him the man most suitable for the job. There's nothing else to it."

He shot Milania a glare that spoke louder than words. *If you get it, then start moving.*

With that, Yulan turned on his heel and walked off. Without thinking, Milania heaved a sigh of relief. His astonishment teetered on the border of respect, but he couldn't quite work out *what* he was feeling. Trailing behind Yulan, he couldn't see the boy's lips moving, nor could he hear the hateful voice that spilled from them.

"I don't intend to play the fool and surrender her to him."

53 Your Voice Reaches

YULAN, WHO WAS ONLY GENTLE toward Violette, and Milania, who was a charitable sort, had left the salon. The only ones in the room now were Violette, who struggled to communicate, and Claudia, who struggled to communicate with Violette.

"......"

"......"

Naturally, this led to a great deal of awkwardness. The air felt heavy and stuffy.

What do I talk about when I'm alone with Yulan?

Violette spoke very little to begin with, so she normally offered the bare minimum responses and allowed Yulan to carry the conversation. Silence often settled between them, but not once did she find it uncomfortable. From that, she'd assumed she was okay with silence, but it seemed to depend on the person she was with. She knew she was supposed to relax during the break, but this was the furthest thing from relaxing.

"That reminds me," Claudia began.

"Y-yes?"

She was momentarily bewildered; she hadn't expected him to initiate a conversation. Hoping she was in the clear, she managed a nod. Claudia's gaze was fixed on the teacup in his hand. He was probably running through his thoughts, stringing his words together one by one. No doubt he was also feeling awkward.

"We have officially adopted the use of tea leaves from Cardina."

"Has the trial period ended?"

"Some people disapproved of its limited availability, but everyone else said that the flavor was good."

Apparently, Claudia had accepted Violette's proposal to switch out the tea leaves relatively easily. The product had to go through a test run first, of course. While those in power often sought out new experiences, they could also shy from change—an outrageous contradiction. Once they became adults, they either adopted a devil-may-care attitude or doubled down on their stubbornness.

Things could be introduced more smoothly in the academy since students were still young and flexible, but some of them still hesitated to give something new a try. Violette couldn't believe that a test run had even happened, let alone that the tea had been officially adopted.

"I haven't been yet myself, but I heard more people are using the salons now," Violette commented.

"Well, it's our duty to know quality, and the change went through without a hitch."

The student council had made out well thanks to her suggestion. As the one who had blurted it out and created more work for them, Violette was delighted that they could now reap the fruits of their labor. She couldn't put a finger on what she was feeling, but she could see that Claudia's lips were curved ever so slightly in a smile, his aura softer now.

"It's all thanks to you, Violette. I appreciate it."

"Oh, no, I didn't really do anything."

"Still, I'm impressed that you even knew about Cardina. I did some research during the trial run, but there's hardly any information on it out there."

"Well, the country *is* a little obscure."

While one might know its name if they studied geography— or if they were someone in Claudia's position—few people had ever actually been there. It was small and lacked any distinguishing characteristics. Therefore, it was strange that Violette knew anything about it.

"Our chef at home often treats us with rare tea blends and exotic ingredients," she explained.

The Vahan household chef had been working there since before Violette was born. He was knowledgeable, skilled in his craft, selective with ingredients, and devoted to inventing new recipes. In the past, he'd also been passionate about nutrition. Back when Violette was a "boy," she disliked him since he tried to feed her incredibly hearty meals, presumably under the order that she receive the exact same meals and portions that her father favored. As he watched the teary-eyed Violette force herself to chew and swallow her food, the chef realized that something had to be done. If he handled this poorly, Violette might end up hating food altogether. It was only a matter of time before her body would begin to reject it.

From then on, he cooked every dish he knew to uncover Violette's tastes: simple dishes, delicacies, even tea and desserts. Violette had already given up on enjoying the taste of food, so the chef started by finding things she could eat without suffering. Bit by bit, Violette began to enjoy her meals. The chef soon had a menu that both suited her palate *and* provided all the proper nutrients. There was a lot she disliked, but little by little he managed to adapt to her preferences.

During these endeavors, the chef learned of Cardina's tea. He heard it mentioned in passing while acquiring ingredients, and he immediately brewed some for Violette.

"It was delicious, and he always let me know right away when we got more."

Now that her father had returned, however, that was no longer possible.

Back when Bellerose was still alive, the chef could spend the house's money for Violette's sake, but now he feared incurring Auld's wrath. Any purchase made to suit Violette's tastes would be criticized, and that criticism turned around into praise for Maryjune nine times out of ten. The people serving Violette understood that if they tried to protect her, it would only cause her more pain. Their hands were tied, and Violette herself didn't want them to try.

Violette knew that giving up was far easier and more peaceful, which was why she'd wished she'd never suggested the tea in the first place.

"I can't believe I can finally drink this tea here at school. I'm glad I recommended it."

Violette always believed that her voice—and by extension, her thoughts and opinions—would never reach anyone. Her screams would be deemed unpleasant and ignored. Only one time in her life did she finally allow those built-up feelings inside her to surge forth, finally letting everyone know what she truly felt...but she didn't realize how pointless it all had been until she was accused of her crime.

Now she had people in her life who not only heard her words but truly considered and even acted on them. Claudia, who she had hurt and manipulated in the past, listened with generosity.

"I'm the one who should be grateful," she said. "Thank you so much."

Violette had committed a crime so terrible that no amount of regret could wash it away, but she still decided not to apologize to Claudia. Instead, she would show her appreciation. Atonement was no grandiose thing, and now she could actually express the thoughts that had grown gnarled and twisted inside her before.

"Ah. Well then...I guess we're even," Claudia managed.

"Oh?"

"I'll accept the gratitude you're offering, so...you should accept mine in return."

Bewildered, she wondered if he was trying to exercise his authority. Looking sullen, Claudia quickly turned away to escape her gaze.

His ears peeking out from the gaps in his hair were dyed a lovely red.

Violette could barely believe the bashfulness he was showing. She wanted to doubt her eyes, yet there he was: flushed scarlet, his eyes flitting back and forth in discomfort. There was a wrinkle in his brow and what almost looked like a pout on his lips. This was a rare sight—it was certainly the first time Violette had ever seen him this way. Once she recovered from the shock, she found herself charmed. A feeling of calm came over her.

Before she knew it, she let out a little "Pfft..."

The noise caught Claudia off guard. "Urk!"

"Pfft... Hee hee! I-I'm sorr—mmf!"

She couldn't contain herself, even when she clapped a hand over her mouth. As she stifled the urge to giggle, she glanced back at his surprised face, losing control once more. Her voice quaked with laughter despite its apologetic tone, leaving it with absolutely no persuasive power.

"Don't laugh, stupid."

"S-sure... Pfft."

"Jeez."

As Violette's shoulders trembled, it was Claudia who broke. His expression had lost its sharpness, and he let out a bitter laugh as if to announce his surrender. He'd given up trying to stop her. Just as he brought the teacup to his lips once more, they heard the click of the door being unlocked.

"We're back..." Milania's voice trailed off. "Um, Mademoiselle Violette, what happened?"

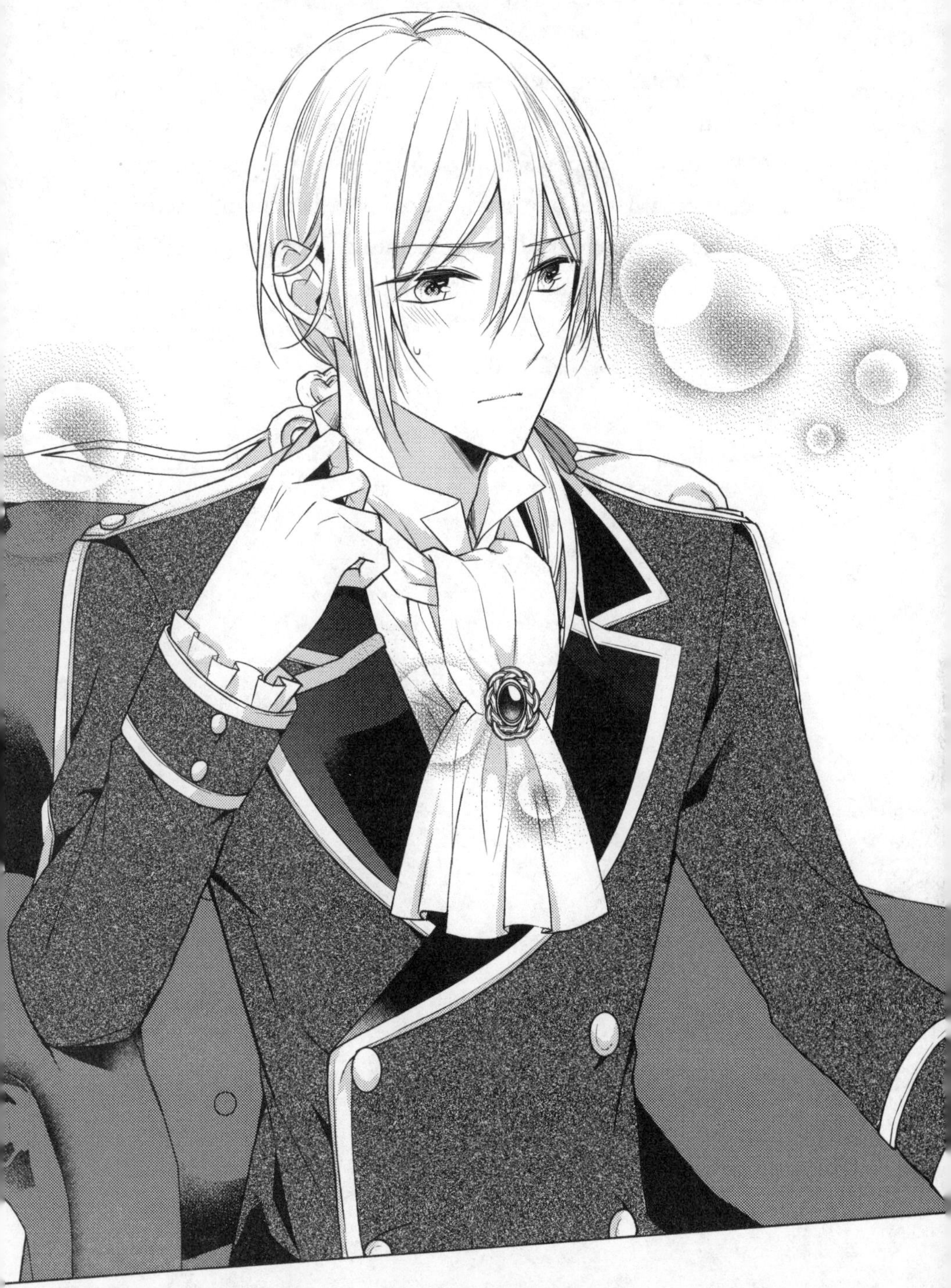

"Vio?" Yulan said, his tone questioning.

"I don't know. Leave her alone," Claudia said.

Milania and Yulan were puzzled at the sight of Violette covering her mouth with one hand to hold back her laughter across from Claudia, who looked utterly bemused.

54   I'd Gladly Fall Into Hell by Your Hand

"**T**HANK YOU VERY MUCH FOR TODAY," Violette said.

"It was nothing," Claudia replied. "I'm sure you could've managed on your own."

"No, it's much easier with someone here to explain it."

As the sky began to darken, their study session came to an end. Once they reached a good stopping place, the four students put away their materials and cleared their writing instruments from the table. Violette and Yulan tucked the exams into their bags and stood up. Violette bowed to the other two, who would be staying behind, but Yulan merely stood there with a fake smile plastered on his face.

"I apologize for taking up your time, Lord Mila," Violette added.

"Be careful on your way home," Milania told her. "Same to you, Yulan. See you later."

"Sorry for taking your time," Yulan echoed. "Excuse us."

In one breath, Yulan magnificently dismissed Milania's words and refreshing smile and spit out a curt reply. He maintained his own smile, but the porcelain perfection of it was frightening.

"Good day to you," Violette said.

After Yulan offered his bare minimum farewell and turned away, Violette trailed behind. When she turned to look at council members once more before closing the door, she met Milania's gaze. Milania looked fairly normal as he waved goodbye, but Claudia, on the other hand, was averting his eyes, giving her a small, awkward wave from shoulder height. It was a pretty amusing sight.

Violette felt a little bud of happiness bloom inside her.

"You're in a good mood," Yulan commented.

"Huh?"

"You've been grinning this whole time."

"No, I haven't."

Despite her words, she pressed her hands to her cheeks. It was normal for people to fret over something others pointed out—this was especially true for Violette, who usually wore an iron mask. She worried that people would think she'd lost it if her stoicism was suddenly replaced with laughter and grins.

But to an onlooker, she looked just as pensive and mysterious as she normally did. Only Yulan could see the cheery smile on her face.

"Did you...have fun?" Yulan asked, his steps freezing.

Violette stopped as well. "Yulan...?"

Though she was facing him now, it was hard to grasp what

he was feeling with his downcast face hidden by his bangs. Yulan normally wore a smile, and his range of expressions was narrow. But what really spoke volumes were his sparkling, golden eyes. Whenever he hid them, it was immediately clear to Violette what was going on inside his head.

"What's wrong? If we don't hurry, the gate will close."

"Hey, Vio." His clear voice trembled slightly.

Normally, calling her name filled him with joy. Nothing in this world elated Yulan more than calling Violette by her nickname, as if to flaunt his sparkling treasure and convey his feelings without a shade of doubt in his heart. It was like his own secret love confession every time.

That was exactly why he didn't want to utter his next words.

"Did you...*enjoy* talking to Claudia?"

As long as Violette was smiling, nothing else mattered. Her smile was the most sacred thing in existence. That was the truth Yulan built his life around. There was nothing more important than Violette's happiness...or so it was supposed to be. That changed the moment he saw Violette laughing freely in front of Claudia.

He didn't mind, as long as Violette was happy. He didn't mind that Violette was laughing.

If it had been anyone else, even Milania, he would have forgiven them. He might not think them worthy of her attention, but he'd still be grateful that they'd delighted Violette.

But Claudia...he couldn't tolerate it from Claudia. That man alone was not allowed.

At a loss for words, Yulan let out a grunt of frustration.

He wanted Violette to be happy. He wanted to lend her his strength. In pursuit of that, he didn't care about his own feelings. That truth hadn't changed. If Violette wished for it, Yulan would go right back to Claudia. They could gather like this again tomorrow. Even now, he remained steadfast—he would do anything for Violette's sake.

That was exactly why Yulan was shaken.

He didn't care about other things. He didn't care about other people. Even Claudia was as important as a pebble on the roadside to him.

But because of Violette, because of *Violette's laugh*, he felt like he was suffocating. A single smile from Violette could send him to heaven...or condemn him to hell.

"Did this...help?" Yulan asked.

For Violette's happiness, Yulan would happily choose hell.

55 | Dreams Are Illusions

Yulan's brow was wrinkled, his eyebrows dipped down, lips pulled tightly together as if he were enduring great pain. He rocked back and forth, swaying. There was no hint of tears in his eyes, but the way his cracked visage had fallen away was as clear to read as any physical sob.

Violette had no idea why he was suffering.

"Yulan...?"

She turned around to see him standing still. He didn't have his usual gentle air around him. His gloom was like a back alley after rain—dark, stagnant, and suffocating, with an atmosphere clotted with moisture and smoke.

"Did this...help?"

Still, he desperately tried to smile through his crumbling mask. He looked like he might collapse at any moment, and his choked words came out like sputtered sobs.

Violette thought Yulan might break.

She knew she had to say something, but she didn't know what. He was clearly hurt, but she couldn't identify the weapon that wounded him. She could forcibly press down on the wound to stop the bleeding, but she doubted that would help. Wrapping a bandage over a thorn prick would only make it fester.

What words would reach Yulan right now?

"It made me happy," Violette began.

Yulan's breath hitched, and he bit down on his lip, tearing into the skin. It was only a matter of time until the blood began to flow.

Even though she didn't intend to hurt anyone, Violette felt crushed by the thought that she had caused Yulan this much pain. She was bad at conversations, her social skills were stunted, and her choice of words deplorable. It was just so difficult for her to express herself.

"It made me happy...that you did all this for me," Violette said.

The wonderful time she had today was a gift from Yulan. Making progress on her studies, seeing a new side of someone unexpected, and the spring in her step were all things Yulan bestowed upon her. She was glad she could speak naturally with Claudia now, but her feelings there were more relief than anything else. Every bit of enjoyment she experienced was all thanks to Yulan. She didn't want his smile to be so sad.

"You did this because you wanted to help me, right? Because of you, I'll be able to sleep well tonight," Violette said. "Thank you." She thanked him from the bottom of her heart, for thinking of her, for wanting to help her, for wanting to be of use to her.

Even now, she didn't know how to convey her feelings properly. It was so rare for anyone to act on her behalf without an ulterior motive. She'd never thanked someone for caring for her like this, either. She'd been drunk on her own misfortune, only seeing herself as a victim without concern for the people who cared for her. She never knew that a thank-you could feel so shallow. Surely just "thanks" wouldn't be enough. She wanted to shove her swirling thoughts deep, deep down inside. Those six letters were far too few, but she was realizing for the first time that she didn't have any other words to offer.

"Thanks," she said again.

Violette stared right into those wavering golden eyes. Yulan had never liked his eye color—he didn't despise it, but it made him feel alienated from her. After all, she knew there was one other victim of the magnetism created by this shiny gold.

Claudia Acrucis.

He was Violette's beloved prince—her first love and the one she dreamed would save her. To the past Violette, this golden color was *his* color. It was the same as a prince's crown: the shining color of the pinnacle. Only during her agonizing days in prison did she realize it was merely a dream to her and a delusion to everyone else.

"They really are beautiful," she said.

"Wha—"

She reached out and touched his cheek, and he didn't recoil from it. When her fingers traced his eyes, the heartbreak stiffening his face turned to surprise.

This gorgeous golden color was the color of the sun, the color of sunflowers stretching out to greet it. It was absolute proof of the crown that charmed everyone. Violette thought it was beautiful. She had chased after this gold, this symbol of the king, in Claudia. Immersed in tragedy, she had sought to become the heroine, although she knew not how to get there.

From the bottom of her heart, Violette felt like a foolish girl. She'd only ever had eyes for the prince. She'd only ever been able to see this color in Claudia. She winced at her own narrow-mindedness. All this time, that color had been so close to her. If she extended her hand, there was someone who was certain to accept it. She wished that she'd realized sooner that the color of the sun was unbelievably gentle.

"This is *your* color."

56 Someone Likened Them to the Sun

VIOLETTE'S SMILE BLOOMED like a flower. But it wasn't her usual smile, reminiscent of roses. This was like a flower bed peppered with small blossoms. Her smile, along with the sensation of her fingers brushing Yulan's cheek, triggered a precious memory. He had cautiously tucked it away long ago so no one could taint it. It was the memory of the one word she said when they met for the first time.

"Beautiful." Right, she had said it back then too.

Until then, he'd hated his eyes and their color. They reminded him and those around him of his upbringing. He despised the royal family, who created and abandoned things as they pleased, flaunting their responsibility without taking care of anything. He hated the golden color that represented them.

"Fake."
"Dirty."

"Muddy."

While the adults held their tongues, children tore through Yulan's defenses with these stinging words. It was common for them to curse at him in public or even gang up on him and pummel him. Being the child of a mistress wasn't usually a problem, but having those eyes certainly was. He was his father's son, yet that fact was heresy where the royal family was concerned. Human sensibilities were a fickle thing.

Yulan's hatred toward his father and his ilk grew and grew, until eventually he detested the entire country. It may have just been a matter of time. His only salvation was the branch family who adopted him, accepting his "abnormality" as a quirk, not a curse. Had he been scorned even in his home, Yulan's young heart would have died. Even so, he had been hurt to the point where he couldn't just accept their love. His character had been permanently twisted.

He managed to stand despite his battered spirit, vowing to make the monsters who had justified his suffering grovel before him. If he cowered in tears like they wanted him to, he would be convicted of a nonexistent crime. These idiots deluded themselves into believing they were heroes, shouldering the populace's expectations and vanquishing demon kings of their own invention. According to them, he simply wasn't normal, and that was all the justification they needed.

Once they defeated him, it would be the end. If he fell even once, they would batter him into the ground. He desperately tried to fight back, but he could only endure, unable to even defend himself. That was the best he could do; the retaliation he wished for was so far outside his grasp. Trying to convince him that he couldn't lose would've been absurd. After all, this wasn't a fight; it was a one-sided beatdown.

Even though he knew his heart was being whittled down, he had no way to recover.

One day, his stress would reach its peak or his mind would break, and then his obstinacy would end. While he was enduring everything with all his might, he was also waiting in a corner of his mind for his heart to fail and his thoughts to stop. He had given up. There would be no change, no end, and no salvation. He couldn't even imagine that someone would come along and take care of everything for him.

"I think they're beautiful," Violette once said.

He had forgotten when exactly he heard these words. He wanted to vividly remember all his memories with Violette, and while he did recall most of them in great detail, the day of their first encounter was blurry. That was back when he was numb and hopeless and could only see things from a detached point of view. He was disappointed in himself, regardless.

Only that scene, that precise moment when her voice first reached his ears, was stored like a photograph down to every last detail. He recalled her short hair and attire, which made her look like a boy at a glance. Even though they were in a dim grove in the shade of a building, she radiated a faint light that gave her a holy air. Her smile was soft, but her gaze was condescending and oppressive as she stared down the bullies around him.

His tormentors lost all their vigor and stood frozen like prey before her.

"Ah, I'm sorry for interrupting your chat. I heard a voice, so I came over," Violette explained.

"Lady Violette," blurted one of the children. "Wh-why are you…?"

"I told you. I heard a voice."

Lady Violette—Lady Violette Rem Vahan. Everyone knew the name of the Vahan family's daughter. For better or worse, she was famous, and she always stood out. In other words, she was the very picture of someone Yulan couldn't deal with.

However, Yulan wasn't the only one shaken by her sudden appearance. Despite the brimming confidence the bullies had shown Yulan moments before, they had suddenly turned into goldfish, flapping their mouths open and closed in wide-eyed stupor. Even Yulan's mind had been kicked somewhere else. That might be why his memory of this time was blurry. Detached, he treated what was happening like someone else's problem. He only realized much later that he was being rescued. Back then, all he wanted was for time to speed up. He didn't stir, lowering his gaze and sealing off his heart.

"Are you all right?" Violette asked.

Yulan hadn't made a peep—the scene was completely silent aside from her voice. She didn't offer her hand, nor did she gently console him. Violette only asked this frank question, and nothing more.

Still, Yulan stayed quiet.

"You're hurt, so you should go to the doctor's office. Unfortunately, I'm not familiar with this place."

She had quickly given up on waiting for Yulan to answer. The way this girl continued the conversation all by herself was anything but normal. Anyone else would relish his lack of response. It was even more likely that they wouldn't have tried talking to him in the first place. He didn't particularly want to be treated gingerly, but it was better than being insulted out of nowhere as he had been so many times.

After some time, he finally spoke up. "You don't hate them?"

"Hm?"

"Everyone says my eyes...are weird... That they're an imitation... They all hate seeing them."

Everyone said so. No matter how kindly he was treated by the family who had raised him, the stones thrown by complete strangers were just stronger. There was nothing scarier to a victim than attacks from a distant, unseen sniper.

His self-directed revulsion stemmed from his growing pile of complexes. He wanted to violently gouge out every instance of that color—but as it was his own body, he stopped himself. He couldn't say when the balance of his emotions tipped and disgust took over.

If they were going to abandon him, he would take that color with him to its destruction.

If they were going to deprive him, he wanted them to tear everything out from the roots.

If they were going to steal from him, he would prefer they just kill him.

If they wanted him dead, he'd rather have never been born.

He did not want this color.

"They aren't an imitation," Violette said.

"Ngh…" Yulan's breath caught in his throat, and his shoulders jerked. Her voice had triggered his fight-or-flight instinct, but it wasn't anger at him that he heard there. When he raised his face, he found himself caught in her glare. The expression didn't frighten him, however. She was glaring at him because she was fighting back her tears. He could tell from the ferocity in her eyes.

"People can only be themselves." She said it slowly, as if to persuade him. "Nobody can be an imitation of someone else."

The words that he had always yearned for were bestowed upon him so painfully and sadly, as if she were crushing her throat and about to throw up blood.

"You're the real you."

"Hrk!"

Yulan felt himself choking up. By the time he realized it, he was sitting down; the strength in his legs had left him. Violette knelt down and finally met him at eye level.

"I'm Violette. What's your name?"

"I-I… I'm…"

His voice dropped off. *Name.* What people called him. His own name. Even though he hadn't forgotten it, he couldn't string the sounds together. An imitation didn't have a name. "Yulan" was the name of a lie. In the softest, most precious spot in his weak heart, he didn't want to be damaged, dirtied, or denied anymore, so his throat refused to part with the word. His fear and vigilance tried to protect the small Yulan's heart. His reservoir of courage had long since dried up.

What should he do? What in the world should he do?!

The more he panicked, the harder it was to talk. If he kept her waiting forever, would he go back to being an imitation? Would the person in front of him who called him real—would Violette start believing he was an imitation too?

He didn't want to cry, but his eyes felt hot. He gritted his teeth so he wouldn't lose to spite, but his determination felt like it would crumble at this very moment. He felt frustrated, bitter, and sad.

Then, just when his accumulated tears were about to spill over...

"You aren't an imitation, so please tell me your name," Violette said.

Her smile was like a blooming flower. While she appeared to look like a boy and spoke in a lower register, her smile was sweet, gentle, and beautiful.

Sugar and spice and everything nice, that's what girls are made of.

That was a nursery rhyme he'd heard from somewhere. He didn't know who had said it to him. It could have been his birth mother, or even his current mother. While he couldn't recall who it came from, he finally realized what it meant.

From that moment on, Violette became the only "girl" in the world to Yulan.

"Yu...lan. It's Yulan...Cugurs."

"Well then, Yulan. I'm going to go eat now. Do you want to join me?"

"Oh... I can come?"

"Of course. I invited you, after all... Unless you don't want to."

"I don't hate the idea..." Seeing that she'd gone ahead, Yulan quickly stood up with a grunt. As he chased after her, he cried, "I'm coming!"

Yulan was small compared to other children his age, so he had a shorter stride and slower walking speed. The distance between the two often grew as a result, and each time, she would turn around and wait for him. He realized a little later that this was love. Back then, he followed her like a younger brother trailing behind his older sister. Still, he always thought it went beyond any normal sister complex—inside, hidden, his heart overflowed with love.

She was an older sister, a savior, a girl, and, unconsciously, his first love.

He just wanted to be by her side. Whenever they saw each other, he stuck to her like a burr. Every time, she smiled at him and accepted him, and every time, his desire to stay beside her grew. He clung on tight, stubbornly refusing to leave.

He loved her, adored her. Yulan's idea of love was Violette. He wanted her to know even a little of his love. He wanted her to accept it. He wanted her to see it and nothing else.

"Nobody can be an imitation of someone else."

He hadn't realized that those words—the ones that saved him—tormented her.

57 | Two

SINCE THAT DAY, Yulan had always watched her. He wanted to devote his whole heart to Violette, the one who saved him. But soon he learned how futile that was and how ignorant he had been.

She had saved him, but he had no way to return the favor. He prioritized staying by her side, but he hadn't done anything for her. Little by little, Violette was warped by her environment. Her beauty wasn't damaged; rather, it became ever sharper. The more she matured, the more she was denied. Given enough time, she might have gone mad.

He wanted to support her. More than that, he wanted to rescue her.

But the one Violette wanted wasn't Yulan.

Love was probably the only thread of hope she had. Whatever was left of Violette's pure heart believed that the prince would swoop in and save her. She dreamed of a fairy-tale ending. Yulan could have dealt with that; if she found someone to save her and make her happy, it wasn't that big of a deal if she chose someone else for the job.

Even after she grew twisted, Violette continued to love Yulan. She doted on him sincerely. It was the only thing that never changed through all those years. And Yulan convinced himself that he was fine with that alone.

⁂

"Yulan...?" Violette said.

He placed his own hand atop Violette's. He held on tight, wishing that she'd never let go, that she'd never *want* to let go. But his wish didn't come true; Violette was just playing along to indulge him. It was no use clinging to someone who wanted to leave him. His behavior was accepted, but his desires were overlooked.

There was no way his feelings would ever come to light. He knew he had to keep up his younger brother act. For Yulan, choosing what was best for Violette was as natural as breathing.

Yet sometimes, even breathing was difficult.

"What's wrong?"

"It's... It's nothing," Yulan said.

Violette cast a doubtful look at him. Something was clearly wrong, but she didn't press the matter any further. With him in this kind of mood, she knew that if she acted suspicious under the pretext of concern, it would backfire.

And she was right—even if she *did* press him for answers, he had none for her. She was the only person he might be able to express these feelings to, but he knew he could never let her know.

TWO

"Let's go, Vio. Miss Marin will be worried if you're late," Yulan said.

"Right."

"And I'm hungry."

"Well, you didn't eat anything during the break."

"I only bought sweets. Whenever I pick stuff for you, I forget about myself."

While they chattered casually, gloom continued to swirl in Yulan's heart. He was supposed to immerse himself in the joy of walking beside her, but he felt like he was watching this scene from a distance.

Yulan knew that his heart was split into two. It wasn't dual personalities or anything of that sort; he simply had one heart reserved for Violette alone and another heart for everything else. The former always took priority. The latter was, essentially, storage—Yulan could live without it if need be. Still, that other heart certainly existed, and it carried Yulan's will. Like anything that existed within Yulan, it would always reflect his love of Violette. Yet among the items haphazardly stashed away there, there was another kind of love. Not love for Violette but the love for Yulan himself.

He desperately wished that it were just the two of them, that they were the only two people in the entire world.

Then Yulan would never know the moment she fell in love with someone else.

I Swear I Won't Bother You AGAIN!

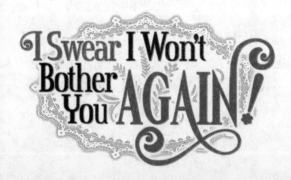

58 | You've Done Your Best

THE VAHAN HOME made Violette more restless than anywhere else in the world, but her room was the only place she could relax. Still, it was a fragile space, a bubble that could pop the moment a member of her family came to visit.

"Are you studying?" Marin asked her.

"Yes, I'm doing a little review."

Violette could usually relax once dinner was over. It wasn't a replacement for their happy family time, but she welcomed these precious moments. She'd only recently realized that being left alone was so much more comfortable because her family held no love for her. But if she could get used to being scorned, to constantly being compared to Maryjune, she could use her alone time to rest up, instead of fretting needlessly over everything that happened.

"Come to think of it, you came home late today as well," Marin observed.

"It's the exam period. I can study better at the academy than at home."

The house was spacious for the number of people living there, and it had a library blessed with a book collection large enough to supply a small shop. It would be the ideal place to study for exams...if her father didn't use it frequently. If they bumped into each other there, she wondered what kind of outrageous, arrogant claims he'd throw at her. She winced just thinking about it.

"I was also with Yulan. I think I'll be returning home around the same time for a while."

"As you wish. Then, starting tomorrow, I shall prepare some midnight snacks for you to nibble on while you review."

"Oh, thank you. But I don't want to gain weight, so could you please keep them minimal?"

"Please tell the chef that, not me."

The servants who had served since Bellerose's time were always looking for chances to spoil Violette. They couldn't offend their employer, and Auld would lash out at Violette if he discovered their favoritism, so they had to be discreet. If they made sweets for Violette, they had to make Maryjune's share slightly larger. If they were washing Violette's dresses, they would do several more of Maryjune's. If they prepared a present for only Violette, then they would have to conceal it so perfectly that no one would ever find out. They exercised so much caution, it was practically overkill.

During these tense days, they could give Violette sweets using the exam period as a reasonable excuse. If they made some for Maryjune as well, that alone could deceive everyone. Even if they prepared only Violette's favorites, they wouldn't be found out. After all, Auld didn't recognize any of Violette's favorite things.

"I'm grateful, but please make them in moderation. Otherwise, I won't be able to eat them all."

"If that pleases you, then certainly."

"I'm not being too pushy, am I?"

"There is nothing more wonderful than seeing our Lady Violette moved."

"Please, all of you...!"

Violette looked astonished, but Marin and the other servants knew that she was genuinely delighted. They had watched her buckle and warp under the venomous influence of her household. As long as they didn't incite her temper, there was no need to worry whether she understood the magnitude of their kindness.

As though out of nowhere, Marin declared, "I shall go and prepare some warm milk for you."

"Huh?"

"Your pen has been hovering around the same place for quite some time, and I see you've been rubbing your eyes. I advise you to rest for the day."

"You were watching?"

"You must be tired. You've seemed more tense than usual today... All that stress isn't good for you."

"You're right... I might have been pushing a bit too hard." Violette had grown desperate after remembering the harm that came from Maryjune's arrival.

Marin could feel a huge difference in the way Violette was tackling her studies compared to last year. She could tell something was out of place. Violette had her own share of troubles back when she was ordered to do exactly as well in school as her father, but once she reached high school, her life as an imitation ended.

"A lot of people went out of their way to help me, so I want to do everything I can."

That was the real reason she was so serious about exams. In the past, she had dug into her studies without asking for help even from Yulan, and yet she still couldn't win against Maryjune. But now that she had this second chance, knowing that she couldn't compete was a blessing. Thanks to Claudia's exam and her knowledge of the likely outcome, she believed she'd perform much better this time around. Now her issue was that she was terrified of wasting the favors done for her. She needed to repay their debt at all costs.

Naturally, she was grateful to everyone for their support, but that wasn't her main reason for working so hard. She was terrified that all this kindness would make her complacent, and she'd have the rug pulled out from under her.

She felt cynical, certain that she would fail once again.

"I can see that you've done your best. If anything, you've gone overboard," Marin told her.

Violette had worked hard to fulfill her mother's wishes. She worked hard to be a good child and earn her father's love. She worked hard to be chosen by the prince. She worked, and worked, and worked... But all of that work warped her. Last time she put her nose to the grindstone in this distorted state, it had been her end.

Violette knew that, to Marin, the current Violette must've looked like she did right before she had broken completely in her past life. Marin would have never imagined that her beloved Violette had come back after failing once, but despite all her struggles her heart was still beating. And now she could make it in time and live without killing her sister. Her instincts had rung the warning bell.

"My job is to allow you some rest after a hard day's work. Occasionally, I might have to pry you away, but I *will* stop you."

"Thanks."

"My pleasure. Therefore, it would be best if you took a break before I have to use *force*."

"Hee hee, I understand. I'll stop here for today."

"I shall get you changed, then."

"I can do it myself. More importantly...can you make sure there's plenty of honey in the hot milk?"

"Of course. Just a moment."

Violette urged Marin to step back before heading to the bedroom. After changing into her nightgown, she untied her loosely bound hair. She had acquired some odd curls, but she could ask Marin to fix them for her later.

A yawn fell from her lips, but no one was around to see it. Violette sat down on her soft mattress and soon found her mind drifting. The feeling she had in this moment was akin to parched earth being quenched. The softness around her made her drowsy.

"I worked...hard."

She knew she'd been working hard, but it didn't occur to her that she'd done her *best* until Marin told her. It seemed that Marin saw it before she did.

"Right... I *did* do my best."

For some reason, that thought brought with it a feeling of relief. As the strength left her body, she surrendered herself, sinking deep into the bed. Tears pricked at the corners of her eyes. It may have seemed foolish to an outsider, but a great weight had been lifted from her heart.

"That's great... That's such a relief!"

No one had ever praised her. No one had ever approved of her. Her parents had only ever denied her. And that made her certain that she was never working hard enough. Sometimes that doubt would push her to exclaim loudly that she'd done all she could and that winning the approval she craved was too difficult. But even when she announced that she'd done her best aloud, a little voice inside her still told her it wasn't enough. She simply couldn't believe that she'd ever done *enough*. So she tried to force the issue, to *demand* the approval she so desired.

She wanted someone to praise her. She wanted someone to tell her, just once, that she'd done well, that she was admirable. The simple words "You can rest already" would have been enough to stop her.

"I did my best. I really gave it my all."

Whether it was from her tears or drowsiness, she no longer knew what she was saying in her hazy consciousness. She only knew that she was muttering the same thing over and over like a broken record.

She didn't know exactly when she fell asleep. She only realized how exhausted she'd been, and how deeply she'd slept, when Marin came to greet her in the morning.

I Swear I Won't Bother You AGAIN!

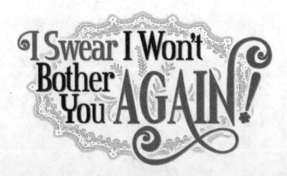

59 A Step Too Far to Keep Her Safe

"PRINCE CLAUDIA, what should I do here?" Maryjune asked.

Claudia began to explain. "Ah, that part would require you to..."

The pair speaking so intimately before Violette looked beautiful; they were a perfect fit for each other. It was like a scene from a fairy tale where the prince and princess cuddle up together. Violette was already well accustomed to the sight.

✦

Everything started the previous morning. Normally, Violette would fade into the background during this happy family time, but today was different. Her attention was about to be wrested away from her delicious breakfast.

"That reminds me," Maryjune said suddenly. "Is it true that you've been attending study sessions after school?"

"Ghk...!" Violette choked on her silky-smooth risotto, then replied, "Yes, I guess."

Having been addressed so abruptly troubled her, but *what* the girl had asked was even more concerning.

"I've been studying in our library ever since I found out that exams are coming up. But I never saw you there, so I wondered why. Then, just the other day, I heard a rumor that you've been studying with Yulan and Prince Claudia."

"That's...right."

Violette's blood ran cold, and her tongue turned to sandpaper. Her hearing, by contrast, became painfully sharp, so that each word from Maryjune rang clearly in her ears. She fought the urge to clap her hands over them.

It wasn't a shock that their time together had sparked gossip. Claudia was always the center of attention at the academy, and Violette stood out as well. Besides, everyone knew that Violette yearned for him. Adding Yulan to the mix, who normally wouldn't dare be seen with Claudia, must've really roused people's curiosity. Still, this was hardly something Violette wanted to discuss at the family table.

"It must be fun to study with friends!" Maryjune said. "You can work together to figure out stuff you don't understand, and you can talk about whatever you'd like during breaks!"

Maryjune had no ulterior motives, and her statement lacked any envious sentiment one might expect to hear. She had only heard the rumor and thought it would make for interesting conversation. The purehearted girl had been raised in a bubble, so she'd never considered speaking around what she really meant. She always said exactly what she wanted.

Violette knew, then, that there was a reason Maryjune hadn't asked to join.

Regardless, someone else sought to give her more than she asked for.

"Maryjune, you can join them starting today," their father stated.

"What?"

"Surely you'll make more progress with them than sitting at a desk by yourself at home. His Highness is excellent, so you can go ask for his assistance."

Frankly, Violette had expected this. After what Maryjune said, *of course* her overprotective father decided to step in. Auld's eyes were soft and filled with love as he watched Maryjune tilt her head in puzzlement. If this was all someone saw of Auld, they would simply see a man who loved his daughter...but only if they didn't see that he'd made his declaration without anyone's permission.

"Please wait," Violette interjected. "Even if she wishes to participate in the study sessions, we haven't yet asked Lord Claudia and the others—"

"This is Maryjune's first test," Auld interjected. "As her older sister, shouldn't you help her?"

His gentle gaze for Maryjune became deadly sharp as it pierced Violette. He was unbelievably single-minded; in his mind, how could Violette exclusively enjoy such a blessing when Maryjune was deprived? While Auld was perfectly rational when it came to his work, his family—that is, his wife and Maryjune—was the center of his world. For the sake of Maryjune's happiness, he would blatantly sacrifice Violette.

"Just because something is fine by you, doesn't mean it's truly fine. I'm sure I've told you to abandon that foolish notion many times already."

"Yes, you're right," Violette said.

She didn't recall him ever saying it, but he probably had. It felt like he was telling her to devote her entire life and everything in it to Maryjune. Her balled-up fist was hot, and her bones creaked with tension. She felt like something had snapped inside her, but she couldn't be bothered to address it yet. The food she'd eaten threatened to come back out; feeling so nauseated, she probably wouldn't be able to eat any more. Even though the meal had been made with her in mind, she didn't have room to think about it.

Violette forced herself to nod. "I understand. I shall appeal to His Highness and the others."

If she rejected him, he wouldn't realize where he'd gone wrong. For someone so fixated on picking apart Violette's behavior to vilify her, he was completely blind to the egotistical nature of his own actions. As he looked down at her with scorn, she imagined he must be satisfied with himself. He was aiding Maryjune, after all—that made any demand both necessary and just.

How nice it must feel to be so naive.

"But it won't be possible today," Violette added.

"What?"

The disdain on his face renewed, but Violette stared back at him coldly.

"This is not a matter I can decide by myself. I need to talk to the other members first and get their approval."

If last-minute cancellations were thoughtless, then the same could be said of last-minute additions. How could one be bad and the other good? People often touted that bigger was better, but the saying fell apart when it came to the size of a crowd. This was a study session, after all—a group effort—and no choice was Violette's alone to make. Thus, she gathered up the sophistry he'd slung at her and returned it right back to him.

"Y-you—"

"I apologize. I'm feeling under the weather, so I shall excuse myself."

She knew from experience that his irritation had swelled into anger, so she stood up before he could explode. Her retreat replaced any sort of genteel farewell she could've offered. She had no interest in what he had to say. No matter what she tried to tell him, there was no way he would ever understand.

I Swear I Won't Bother You AGAIN!

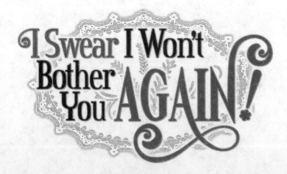

60 | Precipitation

AFTER SCHOOL THAT DAY, Violette told Claudia and the others about Maryjune and got their approval.

She wanted to report to her father that she'd been rejected, but that would only give him another reason to scold her. He may have forced her hand, but he would still be convinced that Violette herself had twisted the proposal to the study group.

Violette never imagined she'd be turned down, of course, but she intended to withdraw the moment they showed even the slightest hint of hesitation. Her father would be upset, but she no longer cared. She was always to blame anyway, so she was prepared for the lectures that would come her way.

Fortunately, everyone had pleasantly accepted...but she still had mixed feelings about it. If they declined, she would have trouble; if they agreed, she would be forced to study with Maryjune. No matter how things turned out, she couldn't win. The fact that she was so used to this frightened her.

"Are you tired, Vio?" Yulan asked. "Should we take a break?"

"I'm fine—and we've only just started. But thanks."

Claudia and Maryjune were chatting so closely in front of Violette, and it made Yulan restless with concern. She knew that he was worried about her. The previous Violette would have certainly cut in between the two, perhaps yelling at Maryjune, to prevent them from getting closer. Now that she had experienced the future, however, she understood that foolish outbursts would only lead to her own torment. Her feelings toward Claudia had changed too, so she didn't feel a shred of jealousy.

"Pardon me, Lord Mila. Is this correct?" Violette asked him.

"Hm? Which one? Ah, yeah. That's fine; you've got it right."

"Thank you very much."

Thanks to Milania, she didn't need to ask Claudia any questions. Claudia was the better student between them, but Violette was excellent in her own way. She was only branded as incompetent because Maryjune was a genius.

"Hey, Vio, let's take that break after all. I'm tired."

"Huh?"

"Let's go get some fresh air, okay?"

"Well, I suppose that's fine."

"All right!" Yulan cheered.

"Lord Mila, will you take a break as well?" Violette asked.

"I...will have to decline. But I'll let Claudia and Maryjune know," Milania told her.

Apparently, their conversation hadn't reached the other two, who were concentrating deeply on their studies. Maryjune was a genius, and so was Claudia. Despite the age difference, a meeting of the minds between them could clearly lead to some constructive conversations.

"Thank you. Let's go, Vio."

"Y-yes..."

Something about the air between Milania and Yulan seemed somewhat prickly—but no, Violette decided that must be her imagination, because Milania's smile remained unchanged. There was no particular affection between the two, but there shouldn't be animosity, either.

Prompted by Yulan, she left the student council room. That alone relieved some of the tension in her shoulders. Whenever she shared a space with Maryjune, she couldn't help but remember that breakfast and grow depressed. Maryjune always reminded Violette of her father. Even though Violette resembled him more in appearance, Maryjune always radiated her father's love.

"Yikes... It's raining pretty hard, isn't it?" Yulan remarked.

In the outdoor passage that connected to the courtyard, the two of them looked up at the sky. It was gray without a trace of blue, though not as dark as night. The current downpour blurred the scene, obscuring their vision and turning the world murky with rain. Violette thought that the sky resembled her hair. This cloudy world suited Violette, and she despised it for that. She hated the rain, scorned the cloudy sky.

"I think people call this 'blessed rain,'" Yulan said.

He giggled and caught a raindrop on his palm. The droplets falling from the edge of the roof plopped onto Yulan's bangs. His smile was joyful and childlike.

"You like rain, huh, Yulan?"

"Hm, I never really thought about it. But I do like the gray sky on rainy days, and I like the sound of the rain and the way it smells. It feels like the world is being washed clean... I hope we can see a rainbow together when it's over."

Yulan was just talking about the rain, but Violette felt like he was addressing her. She desperately wanted to believe that, especially when his smile was so gentle as he spoke.

"Doesn't look like it'll let up anytime soon," she said.

"It feels like we're the only two people in the world. I'm happy."

The sound of falling rain dampened her hearing, so the only other sound was Yulan breathing beside her. There were probably plenty of people left in the expansive building, but the rain erased them entirely.

It really did feel like they were the only ones in the world. There was no one here to deny Violette. Surely, a world with only Yulan by her side would be comfortable. But in such a world, she would be the only one at ease. What of Yulan's feelings? Wouldn't he suffer?

"Being alone with me would be boring."

Her hair, the same gray as the world around them, covered her face as she looked down. Its color was dimmer than dim and dull even in the light. Suddenly, a large hand brushed that hair aside, tickling her ear. Now that her line of sight had been broadened, she saw the sun in the middle of the rain.

"It would make me the happiest man in the world."

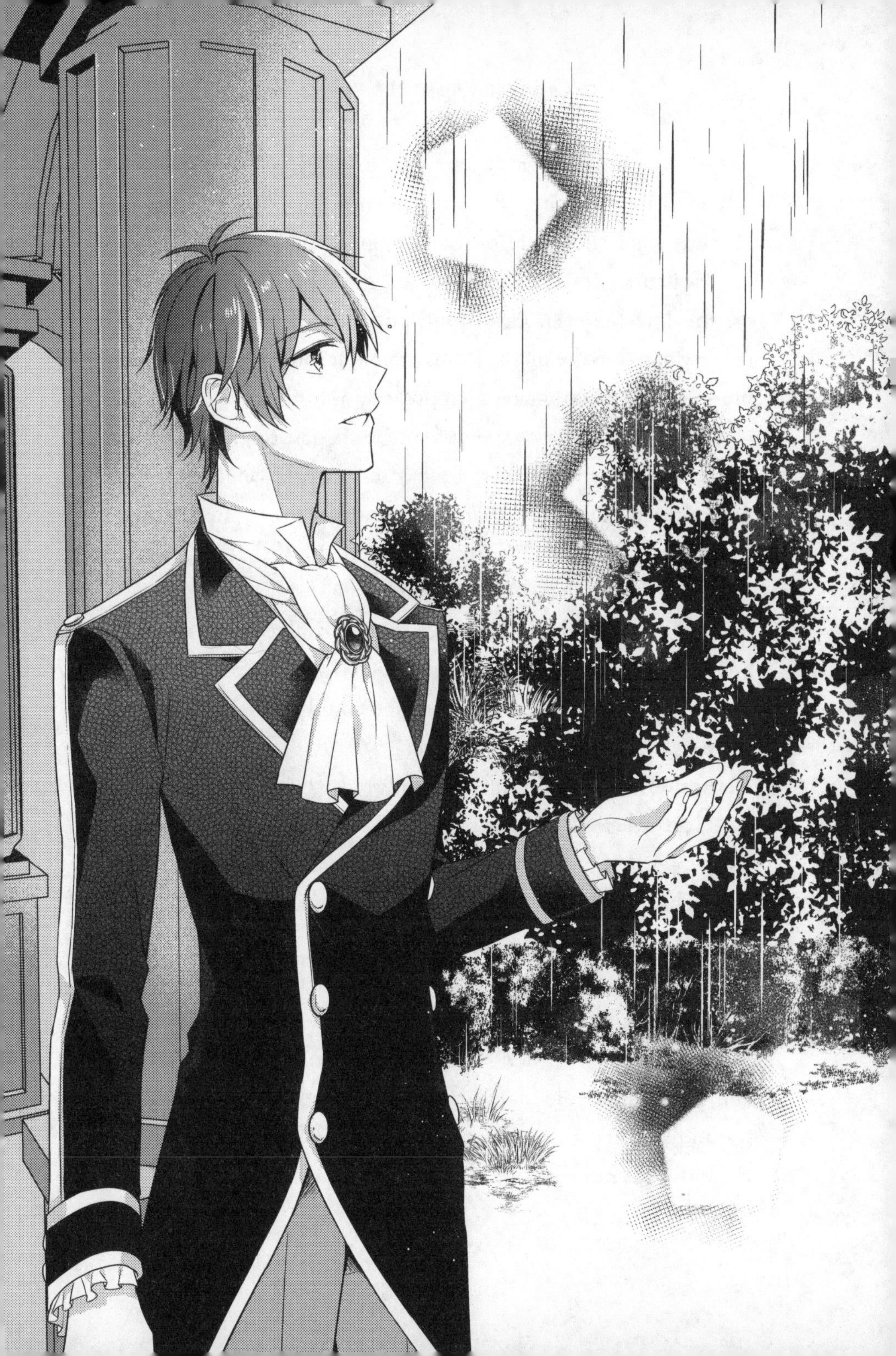

His eyes crinkled as if from the brightness. His hand was extended as if in desire. His smile was more beautiful than gentle, as it was when she saw it for the first time.

Moisture glinted in her eyes, and in that moment she stood on the line between childhood and maturity. Her youthful naivety dared to dream of the unattainable, but she knew in this moment how unattainable that dream was for her.

And anyway, that dream was a mere suggestion to her; a fleeting fancy that would never come true. A world where only the two of them existed together was practically a fairytale. It could never occur in the real world. In spite of all of that, it was the greatest utopia Yulan could imagine.

Violette was speechless. Her eyes were like the raindrops bouncing off the leaves as they opened wide in surprise. Yulan's statement was so unexpected that she couldn't infer the deeper layers of meaning.

Seeing her reaction, Yulan carefully redrew the line in his heart.

He'd resigned himself to the role of her younger brother, but he worried it meant that when the time came, she wouldn't accept his protection. So he set himself a goal to slowly change Violette's perception of him.

Little by little, he'd crafted a more masculine image, so carefully and gradually that these new elements of his personality would slip right past her. He layered them on top of each other and hoped that someday, when he was ready, his full feelings would reach her.

Now was not that time.

"Shame that happiness won't last once we go back to the salon," he joked. His tone was casual, his expression softer now. Luckily, it was easy for Yulan to don an innocent face.

He brought his hands together and stretched his arms over his head. Yulan was so tall that furniture meant for the comfort of others always felt a little cramped. His joints would get stiff as he unconsciously hunched over.

"Guess we should head back now," he said. "If we stay here too long, we'll freeze."

"Oh...right." Violette was still in a daze.

"Would you rather not go back yet? Should we look for another library?"

Yulan's mind immediately jumped to Claudia and Maryjune. He didn't know if seeing them together was painful for Violette or if Maryjune alone was the problem, but if she didn't want to go back, he would take her elsewhere. If they stayed here, the wind and rain would get to them, but they could easily find a spot indoors. Any libraries or salons far away from the student council room would work. However, his plan was halted by Violette's next words.

"N-no, that's not it," she told him, sounding flustered.

Yulan gave her a questioning look.

"I...wanted to apologize to you."

I Swear I Won't Bother You AGAIN!

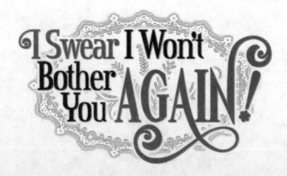

"H<small>M</small>?"

An apology meant asking for forgiveness and making amends. The concept was simple enough, but Yulan felt totally lost. Violette herself was struggling to get her thoughts together; her eyes wandered and her fingers were stiff. Her resolute attitude hardly ever crumbled; it was rare to see her in this state.

"Um, did I do something again?" Yulan asked.

"No, not at all..."

Unable to explain herself properly, Violette regretted speaking up. She wanted to apologize for Maryjune's sudden appearance. Her father's ultimatum had angered her because Yulan had set all this up for her. She knew how Yulan felt about Claudia, so she understood how difficult it must have been for him to ask for this favor. It had made her incredibly happy, and she'd wanted to do what she could to repay him.

But her father didn't have a shred of consideration for Yulan's efforts or Violette's gratitude. His words were law. Violette could tolerate his insults, but she had to object when it became more than that. And in this case she felt that he wasn't only looking down on her but also Yulan.

Now that she was with Yulan, her anger had simmered down into guilt. She wanted to apologize for her father's rudeness, for getting Yulan involved in their family issues and for making him crush his heart beneath his own heel. But when she tried to put it into words, she had to chide herself for being so thoughtless.

"Um... It's about Maryjune."

"Oh, that doesn't bother me. I'm not the one teaching her, after all."

"Ah, yes... That's true."

Of course Yulan would say that. Still, Violette couldn't feel satisfied with how easily he brushed the matter away until she thought it through for herself. Violette had blundered ahead, powered by her own guilt, but Yulan hadn't been there to hear her father's words. If Maryjune had brought up the matter to him, she'd surely have left out much of the nuance. Maryjune always assumed good faith from her father, since his words came to her swaddled in complete parental love. If Yulan had heard Maryjune's explanation for joining the study group it wouldn't contain Violette's discomfort, nor her guilt, nor the context that led her to apologize now.

Which meant there was no need to purposely tell him everything and make him feel uncomfortable. Luckily, it didn't matter if Violette's odd behavior stood out to Yulan. She hadn't let slip any of what she'd originally meant to say, and so long as she could fool him, he surely wouldn't pry any further.

"Well, as long as you're fine with it. I was just a little worried since I suddenly brought in another person."

She wondered if she was smiling properly. The corners of her mouth were raised, but that was it. She lowered her face as much as she could, hoping to hide her expression. She'd rather he only see through the gaps in her bangs than scrutinize her clumsy smile.

"I'm sorry for keeping you. If we don't hurry back, our study session will be nothing but break."

She wondered how long it had been since they left the salon. If they were gone for too long, they would forfeit valuable study time. Their absence might become a cause for concern, and Violette dreaded to imagine the sort of problems her kind-hearted half sister would create.

Violette lightly touched Yulan's arm and prompted him to return, hoping to walk right past him. No matter what expression she wore, she wouldn't be found out.

Just then, his warm hand reached out and grabbed hers to stop her.

She let out a little noise of surprise as she nearly fell over. Her body was lightly tugged backward, and the back of her head touched something solid yet warm. Whatever it was that supported her did so with a touch lighter than air. But before she could look up, a voice sounded from above her.

"I'm fine. I'm really fine."

Violette couldn't bring herself to reply. She was being hugged, but lightly; he had pulled her body close, but his arms weren't wrapped around her waist, and she wasn't clinging to him, either.

It was just a light touch; she felt only the faintest meeting of body heat.

"I'm much bolder than you give me credit for," Yulan told her. "And I'm not about to get my feelings hurt, either."

That young, wounded Yulan who had been on death's door no longer existed. Since the day Violette saved him, Yulan's heart had grown stronger. While Violette still doted on him like a younger brother, he had grown bold enough to receive her pampering without worrying about what others would think. He didn't care at all about those lowlifes, their impressions, or their words. If Violette was fine, if she allowed it, if she accepted it, then it was fine. Nothing else mattered.

He added, "I'm okay. Thanks for worrying about me."

Yulan couldn't guess what Violette was thinking or what she was worried about. Rather, he only had a slight inkling. All he knew was that she felt somewhat indebted to him over the matter with her half sister. But Violette didn't need to worry about a thing. In Yulan's eyes, Maryjune was as worthless as a pebble on the road.

A pebble that proved a problem to Violette would be eradicated without question. But if Violette was out of the picture, Yulan didn't have a speck of interest in Maryjune. If anything, Maryjune's presence was a good thing, since it meant Yulan didn't have to see Violette and Claudia acting like a couple.

"I don't care about anything as long as I get to study with you. It doesn't matter to me if other people come or go." Despite the deep truth of that statement, he kept his tone light.

Violette was silent, her eyes downcast. She gently pushed against his shoulder and returned the space between them. She unfastened his hand from hers, stood beside him without looking at his face, and began to leave. The two of them walked at the same pace.

"I know you're bold, Yulan," Violette said.

"Oh, do you now? Whatever you're thinking, I'm ten times that."

"A humble person wouldn't impose upon the prince."

"Are you still upset about that?"

"I'm grateful for what you did, but it still scared me to death."

"Then it sounds like I have no reason for reflection or regrets!"

"Not even a *little* reflection?"

Their conversation was casual as always; there wasn't a trace of the intimacy they'd just experienced. Violette accepted everything Yulan offered her. After all, his affection for her wasn't anything unusual.

Nevertheless, the darkness nesting in Violette's chest felt a little lighter.

I Swear I Won't Bother You AGAIN!

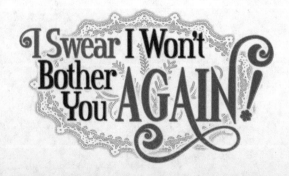

62 Touching Now

WHEN YULAN AND VIOLETTE returned to the salon, they were greeted by an unexpected scene.

"You're back?" Claudia said.

"Oh, Your Highness..." Violette said.

On the table closest to the door lay Violette and Yulan's untouched study materials. Farther in was the table Maryjune and Claudia had been using. The room was large and those tables were far apart, but both could be seen from the entrance. For some reason, Claudia was sitting at *their* table—in what had been Milania's seat.

That wasn't all. Claudia was the only person there. No Milania, and no Maryjune.

"Um, where are Lord Mila and Maryjune?"

"In the library," Claudia answered. "Maryjune was unfamiliar with parts of our curriculum, so the library is better suited to fill in those gaps."

"Is that so?"

Violette understood what Claudia was saying. Just because Maryjune was a genius, it didn't mean that she would be able to adjust to a new environment without issue. This academy was remarkably different from the average school, and it was expected that she would stumble over aspects she'd never encountered as a normal student. She could study from someone's past exams in the salon, but the library was a better place for her to acquaint herself with the curriculum.

"Um, then why are you here, Your Highness?" Violette asked.

"If I had gone with them, you two would be locked out of this room."

"No, that's not what I meant."

Claudia tilted his head, puzzled.

Violette reined herself in before her tone could grow forceful. It wasn't Claudia's fault that he couldn't understand her. The misunderstanding was hers.

The thing that surprised her wasn't that Claudia was here...but that he had allowed himself to be separated from Maryjune. Of course, one of the student council members would have to stay behind, but she would have absolutely expected Milania to stay instead.

Violette wondered if something had happened while she and Yulan were taking their break. When everyone was present, they split into a pair and a trio. Before, Claudia was the one who'd been teaching Maryjune, and he'd appeared to be enjoying himself. While this might've been a preconceived notion on Violette's part due to her memories, she thought it apparent that the two were attracted to each other. Yet, for some reason, the group had decided that Milania and Maryjune would pair off.

She managed to say, "I mean, shouldn't you have gone with Maryjune?"

Claudia didn't seem to follow. "Are you saying you'd rather that Mila had stayed behind?"

"Not at all! It's just—"

Yulan cut in. "You were the one teaching Maryjune, so you should have accompanied her to the library instead of Lord Mila."

Violette had been struggling to explain, so Yulan's explanation was a lifeline. He smoothly stepped in front of Violette, and now she couldn't see his face. Standing before Claudia, Yulan's smile looked far more forced than usual; his eyes alone betrayed his lack of self-confidence.

Claudia had trouble dealing with Yulan, and he didn't have the best impression of Violette, so nothing about his waiting behind for them seemed normal.

"My original promise was to oversee Violette's studies," Claudia replied.

Promise... Indeed, that was what Yulan asked of him. Yulan viewed Claudia as an enemy, but despite his reluctance, he'd entrusted the prince with this very task.

"Violette asked us to allow Maryjune to participate, so I taught her the basics," Claudia went on. "That should be enough."

His words were spoken matter-of-factly. Claudia didn't seem to have anything against Maryjune, but it was still strange that his attitude toward her wasn't more positive. Maryjune's angelic smile could enamor anyone who saw it, after all. The girl's best qualities were her personality and general air. That was entirely detestable to the Violette of the past, but now she couldn't care less who the girl charmed.

Still, Violette had assumed it was that charm that attracted Claudia to Maryjune.

Is it because they just met? Last time, it was practically love at first sight.

Claudia had chosen Violette. A simple truth, but one that had shocked her to the core. The old Claudia had been quite single-minded. His pursuit of Maryjune in the previous timeline was sincere, but admittedly, he was the sort of man who could be spurred to act by one strong emotion.

Violette's past self had seen Maryjune as an enemy and tyrannized her because of it. She loathed her, hated her, and really, *truly* wanted her dead. And Claudia's fervent adoration for the girl had been the origin of her swelling hatred. He thought only of Maryjune, so of course he detested Violette. Through her desire to steal his heart, Violette's tempest of hate had grown more and more violent. During the worst of it, she couldn't access even a fragment of Claudia's affection for herself.

She couldn't bring herself to reply.

"Violette...? If you'd prefer Mila, I can go switch with him right now." Claudia offered her an apprehensive smile.

"Ngh! N-no! You're...quite all right, Your Highness."

"That's good to hear."

It was completely bewildering, but he truly had chosen her over Maryjune. But whether his feelings had yet to sprout or he felt obligated to fulfill his promise, Violette was certain this wouldn't last forever. In that case, she wanted to enjoy this blessing while she could. Claudia was an excellent teacher, after all; he was smart and could answer her questions quickly. Mila was a good option too, but there was no need to request a switch if Claudia was willing to work with her.

"Let's get started, then. How far did you get with Mila?" Claudia asked.

"Ah, right."

She walked past Yulan and sat down in her seat. The arrangement of her textbooks was untouched from when she left.

"We made it to here before I took a break."

"This'll be next, then. Did you have trouble with anything?"

"Lord Mila went over everything, so I should be fine."

"You didn't find his explanations hard to understand?"

"I don't think so...? I got them right away."

Yulan stared at the two of them as they naturally slipped into conversation. Violette didn't notice as her back was toward him, but Claudia sensed it as soon as Yulan raised his head. He stole a quick glance at the unmoving shadow.

The prince murmured, "Huh?"

Were those eyes gazing at him with a passive, baleful loathing? Or was this a frosty stare intended to pierce him to the core? Claudia could read one emotion into that intense look for certain: disgust. There was no way Yulan would ever accept Claudia talking to Violette. His expression now was devoid of any kindness. Anyone would be a fool to expect anything else.

"Vio, scooch over a little more," he said, almost playfully. "I can't sit down."

"Oh, I'm sorry."

"I'm the one who should be sorry; I'm taking up your spot."

"It's fine. You need more space than I do."

Yulan flashed the sort of smile that most people would find pleasant, and Violette's expression softened, too, into something more tender than the one she wore when talking to Claudia. The prince was already familiar with their relationship; it was common to witness the two of them chatting casually both in school and during high society gatherings. Seeing Yulan's blissful smile made Claudia second-guess what he'd seen a moment ago. But he wasn't mistaken; it hadn't been his imagination.

A moment before, this man had looked like a lost child about to burst into tears.

63 I Won't Pray to God

EVEN IF THERE WERE MORE members of their study group now, the actual tasks hadn't changed. Their progress hadn't been helped or hindered. Just as Claudia had said, teaching Maryjune the basics had apparently been enough. She barely asked any questions and worked silently by herself. Claudia, for some reason, left Maryjune to her devices and stuck with Violette instead. He'd said this had to do with his promise to Yulan, but Violette couldn't let her guard down. This Claudia was too different from the one in her memories.

She already knew how the tale of her unsightly love ended. After she was done reaping everything she had sown, none of her love or even regret remained. Still, she couldn't lie to herself and say that she wasn't hurt by the way he'd looked at her, gaze full of contempt.

But the Claudia from the past was gone. Violette already knew that her memories were useless in this rewound world. If she tried to anticipate and avoid a dire outcome, she would be swatted by some new misfortune. She knew she had to separate this new Claudia from the old one she remembered.

Still, she couldn't forget the way those scornful eyes looked down on her.

Was I expecting him to return my feelings all along?

If she could fully abandon her feelings toward him, her memories, and everything else, then adapting to her current circumstances would be simple. At this point, she should have no expectation of any warm feeling from him, so she shouldn't be hurt. Why couldn't she let go? Why was she still fixated on Claudia's gaze?

Maybe she was just clinging miserably to her squashed hope. Even in the face of her new indifference, she couldn't rule that out.

That's not good. I'll only end up repeating my mistakes.

When the worst-case scenario crossed her mind, she brought a hand to her forehead and her head drooped. If she went down that road, this incredible chance to redo her worst mistakes could turn into an encore performance. That painful year of experience would be for naught.

Living through that hopeless ending once was more than enough.

She shook her head several times, as if to shake off her hopes, and the motion made her a bit queasy. If such a feeble motion could realign her heart, then it was painfully weak. However, the gesture—which normally would've been ignored—was powerful enough to elicit the concern of a passerby.

"Um... Are you feeling all right?" someone asked.

"Huh?"

"You seem distressed."

A young lady appeared, adorned in lovely purple hues that gave her a noble look. Her hair was dark violet, while her eyes were light. Neat, lovely, and elegant—such pure descriptors suited her, so everyone called her a saint. When Violette looked at this student up close, she found herself agreeing. This beautiful, immaculate being was like a Casablanca lily personified.

This was Rosette Megan, an international student like Gia and princess of a neighboring country.

Rosette's brow furrowed, and Violette couldn't help but think that when trouble was written on the faces of beautiful people, it raised more concern than necessary. Even more so if they were gentle and pure.

"If you're finding it hard to walk, I can call for someone," Rosette said.

"Oh, no, I'm fine. I was just thinking about something."

"I...see. Then I apologize for interfering."

"Not at all. I'm sorry for worrying you."

"Please, no need."

The princess smiled and walked away, leaving behind the scent of flowers. Even her exit demonstrated her incredible grace. Like Violette, Rosette attracted onlookers wherever she went—though the gazes aimed at Rosette never held a hint of malice, while the ones Violette received were tainted by sensationalized rumors. Those who looked at Violette were seeking something from her bewitching allure, evaluating her pedigree, or considering their suspicions of her stepmother and half sister.

I'm not really envious of her, though. It's all the same when you're under observation.

Violette would've preferred the gazes of adoration and respect directed toward Rosette several times over, but being stared at felt the same in the end. Ideally, she'd want to be invisible, much as she knew that wish was absurd.

People avoid talking to me now, so I'd say I have it better.

People adored Rosette, so they tended to gather around her. Conversely, people often distanced themselves from Violette due to the unsavory rumors and her unapproachable aura. If Violette was going to draw attention at all, her current situation had its advantages.

People would never feel the same way about her that they did Rosette. Both the past and present Violette were far from noble and upright.

"Noble and upright, huh?" she murmured.

She had given up on her family, but that didn't mean she'd forgiven them. She couldn't genuinely love Maryjune or let go of the pain her father caused. Knowing that resentment was meaningless wouldn't erase her grudges. If she couldn't bare her fangs, her emotions would eventually explode at her father. In the end, even if she had changed her ways, nothing about Violette's temperament was any different.

It's almost like I'm taking advantage of God.

It wasn't a desire to serve God that inspired her to become a nun; it was simply the easiest way to run away from her family and home. She'd go back on her claim that she could endure any lifestyle better than her intolerable home life and instead use God as an excuse to build herself a reasonable life. Any devout follower would fume with rage.

Once upon a time, she'd thought that God had saved her. She thought that everything she had now was a chance gifted to her by God... Or at least, that was what she'd tried to believe. But there was no need to for her to pray for salvation. She didn't believe in fairy tales, or shooting stars that would grant one's greatest wish.

She may have said her new chance was all thanks to God, but she couldn't quite believe it.

I might not believe in God at all.

I Swear I Won't Bother You AGAIN!

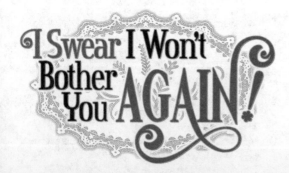

Side Story - Christmas, Part 1

EVERY YEAR, a holiday known as Christmas was celebrated throughout the world. It was a grand day of tradition and festivities that extended...to Violette's own home, apparently.

There was a reason for the unsure comment—Violette alone didn't know it was the holiday until the day itself arrived.

She only realized what day it was when she left her room to go eat breakfast and found that the hallway had been transformed overnight. At this time of year, the world was decorated with three colors: red, white, and green, vibrant shades whose contrast was all the more apparent as she stepped from the darkness into the light.

Oh, I guess today's Christmas.

She was acquainted with Christmas in her way. The academy had gone into full Christmas mode. The cityscape had already transitioned to match the holiday some time ago, and she had attended Christmas parties in the past. It was generally celebrated everywhere except for in her own home.

"We had these ornaments in the house, huh?"

Well, her father might have brought them from another residence. Perhaps he celebrated Christmas there. In any case, tonight's dinner was likely to cause a fuss.

Soon after leaving her room, Violette saw Marin walking toward her. Marin had immediately noticed Violette and picked up her pace—though her steps still made no noise.

"Hello, Lady Violette."

"Marin, you're just in time."

"I apologize for my lateness in greeting you this morning."

"I came out earlier than usual, that's all. Is it that time already?"

"Oh. Um, about that... Why don't I serve you today's breakfast in your room?"

"Hm?"

She'd assumed that Marin had called out to her because breakfast was ready, but looking at Marin's scrunched-up face, she realized that wasn't the case. A morning alone in her room would be welcome, but she still felt wary; not of Marin but of the other members of her household.

"Did something happen?" Violette asked.

"No, nothing. But...it's Christmas Day."

Violette gave her a quizzical look. She didn't understand what Christmas had to do with it. Many people, especially children, considered this event quite enjoyable, but it was nothing more than an ordinary day to Violette.

Apparently, it would not be an ordinary day this year.

"The master wishes to finish his work early, so he will not be attending breakfast. And the madam and Lady Maryjune have plans to go out for breakfast."

"Aah."

Violette understood the situation and Marin's suggestion. This maid truly, deeply understood her mistress's heart. If her father wasn't going to be present and the other two had plans, then Violette had an easy excuse to be absent from the breakfast table. Even if the two ladies waited for her, they would likely prioritize their own plans if she lagged behind. But if her father heard that she appeared and then left the breakfast table, it would be terribly troublesome.

"I believe there will be a Christmas dinner tonight, so it would be best for you to rest now," Marin said.

"I see."

Although Violette had expected this, Marin's pained expression told her she would be swallowing tonight's dinner without tasting it.

"May I ask you to provide an excuse for me, then?"

"I've already given them one: 'Her condition is poor, so she'll rest until dinner.'"

"You didn't think I might attend?"

"I intended to take forceful measures if by some chance you decided to."

"You say some scary things sometimes."

They were joking around, but there was truth underneath it. Marin knew that the chance of Violette declining her proposal was nonexistent.

Once Violette accepted her offer, she turned right around and made the extremely short walk back to her room. She had already changed out of her loungewear, but now she had the chance to eat both breakfast *and* lunch in her room thanks to Marin. She imagined she'd feel more comfortable if she changed back into it.

"Marin looked busy," she mused.

Marin usually worked exclusively for Violette, yet she appeared to be running all over the place today. Well, it was House Vahan's first Christmas. The servants who had worked in the other residence were probably accustomed to the expected tasks, from decorations to dinner preparations, but there had been no celebrations here in the main house. The servants must have worked in such a panic to adorn its many rooms and hallways, since it was so much larger than the other residence. It made sense that they would need the help of all available staff.

She'll be bringing me breakfast too. The least I can do is dress myself.

Violette was perfectly capable. Outside of party dresses, even a child could change their own clothes.

"Wonder where I put the new ones." Dressing herself wasn't a problem, but finding her new loungewear in the excessively large walk-in closet might be. The closet was spacious enough to befit the huge mansion to which it belonged.

Although many aristocrats always had their servants dress them, Violette handled most of it herself because of the environment in which she was raised. She did whatever she could to lighten Marin's workload. Still, Marin generally handled the preparation of Violette's clothes and the management of her closet. Since laundry was one of Marin's duties, it was more efficient that way. Even so, Violette's unfamiliarity with the location of her own clothing made her feel thoroughly pathetic.

"I don't think it'll be too far in, though."

Brilliant dresses and gorgeous pieces of jewelry filled the space, but her plain clothes and loungewear had to outnumber them—those were the items she used most often, so they should have been easy to find. She ended up restlessly moving around in her closet, feeling like a thief even though everything belonged to her.

"Oh."

She stopped at a corner filled with dresses. Several identical uniforms were lined up here. Judging by the dresses and coats hanging on hangers, this had to be where her uniforms and casual clothes were stored.

"Around here, maybe?"

From what she could see at a glance, the outfit she was looking for wasn't hanging up. In that case, it would be in the drawers alongside the undergarments. Violette opened each drawer, took a glance at the neatly arranged clothing inside, and shut it again. She scoured them from top to bottom until she finally found what she was looking for.

"Here it is."

The moment she opened the drawer, the soft scent of flowers wafted through the air. The clothes were freshly washed with her favorite fabric softener. She'd previously thought all the clothes inside were the same because they had the same manufacturer, but when they were folded and lined up like this, she could see they were all different. She had always let Marin choose her clothes, and she couldn't decide what to wear when the whole stack was presented to her.

This one's red and white...

A dark-colored outfit peeked out from the bottom of the stack. It was soft and subtle, but the color combination stood out among Violette's collection. That was probably why it had been pushed into the depths of her closet, but for some reason, she felt like bringing it out today. Maybe because the whole house was filled with Christmas spirit.

She reached out and tried to take it without disturbing the clothes on top. However, Violette was the daughter of an aristocrat; she normally never did something like this and couldn't imagine the consequences. Forcefully yanking out the bottom item had an obvious result.

"Ah—!"

All the other clothes spilled out.

"Oh, no... Now I've done it."

She let out a sigh, knowing she had brought this on herself. Half the contents of the drawer had been launched past her, but the clothes would be easy enough to pick up and put away.

She was looking around to collect them when she noticed something sparkling brilliantly in the corner of her eye. She'd only expected her dresses to glitter, so she wondered if some accessory had slipped between the gaps of the scattered clothes.

"This is…"

In her hands was a small hoop decorated with green and silver ribbon. It was a palm-sized version of the ornaments seen so frequently during this festive season, but that was precisely why it stood out in this house…and especially in her room.

"A Christmas wreath?"

The item, wrapped in transparent vinyl, was stained in several places and seemed quite old. It appeared to be handmade, somewhat crooked in shape and with a few more ribbons than the ready-made ones.

Such a thing shouldn't have existed, but there it was in Violette's hand. She gingerly touched the outer ribbons. The dirty parts probably couldn't be scrubbed clean. She wondered how long it had been here.

The sight triggered a distant memory.

"Oh! I know what this is."

She remembered that day—a day sacred in her mind. Something had happened on that day for the first and last time. It was the only Christmas Violette had ever experienced.

I Swear I Won't Bother You AGAIN!

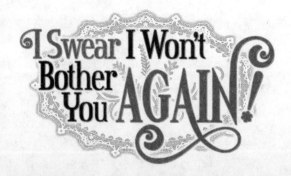

VIOLETTE COULDN'T RECALL how many years it had been. It happened before her mother was bedridden, back when Violette was not yet living as a girl. It was just around the time when Violette suspected she could no longer pass as a boy, and Marin had already begun working at the mansion.

On Christmas Day, there were large parties at everyone's houses. She couldn't remember whose house she was in or what sort of people attended. However, during that time in her life, Violette cherished any time when she could be away from her mother and temporarily return to being a girl.

Wearing a dress again, being a girl, and high society—all these obligations felt constricting and unavoidable, but what she dreaded the most was the sight of her father's bitter expression after all this time. His face was cold, as if he had no interest in her whatsoever; yet even so, some dissatisfaction rose in his eyes when he looked at her dressed up. Now that she thought back on it, he had probably been picking her apart, frustrated that it was her instead of his beloved Maryjune. Even though he had no interest in Violette and her elegant outfit, he resented the fact that Maryjune couldn't dress that well. That was just the sort of man he was.

Nevertheless, while she was here, Violette had to act like the proper daughter her father needed to display. And when she returned home later that day, she would have to endure her mother's sharp gaze and fearsome wrath over the time she'd spent being feminine.

To Violette, high society was a special kind of hell that made everyone trapped there irrational. It didn't matter what excuse they used for this party—the Spirit of Christmas or Santa Claus, it didn't matter—it would end up painful for her either way. She would have to share this space with her father and then enter another ring of hell when she returned home. Violette didn't want to stay any longer, but she also didn't want to hurry home faster. There was no end in sight to her torture.

At least, that was the kind of day it was supposed to be.

"Found you, Vio!"

"Oh, Yulan."

"You're really good at hide-and-seek. I was searching for you the whole time."

"You say that, but you always find me."

"Hee hee hee."

Yulan's cheeks were tinged red, his breathing faintly ragged. He was still young, but he'd lost most of the plump baby fat he'd had when they first met. The visible differences brought about by their one-year age gap must have lessened before she realized it.

Now the only difference between them was that Violette was taller. As a boy, Yulan would grow bigger in the future, and while Violette would also grow up, she wouldn't be able to hold her lead for long. The difference in their sexes would be clear soon, especially since girls grew quickly.

At that time, Violette had begun to attend more social events in dresses. Her femininity had always shined through even during her constant cross-dressing. When had her mother begun to notice that? Could that unstable person endure seeing her daughter walk her proper path to womanhood?

Violette had known for a long time that she couldn't become a boy. She had no desire to be one, so faking it made her resentful. Still, she was terrified of becoming a girl again too. Though born as her daughter, Violette's mother had given strict instructions that Violette would become a boy and a living copy of her father. Her life's path had been crushed. But the path she should have taken was still there waiting for her, beyond the wreckage of the crushed one.

When she resigned herself to thinking and acting like a boy she felt bitter, but it was also strangely comfortable. As long as she did what she was told, she wouldn't experience any more pain or suffering. But she couldn't bring herself to obey any longer. Her body was beginning to mature no matter how much she or her mother willed it not to.

"You don't look so good," Yulan remarked. "Are you okay?"

"Oh, I'm fine."

Her adorable friend, who she treated like a younger brother, was looking at her with a face full of worry. He could smile now, but she knew the pain he harbored deep inside. She wanted to smile back at him even if it meant concealing her own agony. She still wanted to be a dependable older sister who Yulan could look up to.

"Hey, Vio... Do you know what day it is?"

"What day is it?" Violette parroted back.

"It's Christmas."

"Of course I know that."

They were standing in the middle of a party that had been decked out in so much Christmas-colored finery that at the merest glance it screamed "Christmas party."

"They say that Santa comes on Christmas. If you're a good kid, Santa'll bring you happiness," Yulan said.

"Yes, that's right."

Violette offered a vague smile, so Yulan laughed shyly and averted his eyes.

Santa will bring you happiness.

It was a line from a picture book everyone knew. Even Violette was aware of the happy story where the cute, jolly Santa Claus bestowed mountains of smiles. Many children read it over and over again, believing in Santa and holding on to their dreams.

Violette could not be one of them.

Not only had Santa never visited her, but Violette had never spent this day thinking it felt like Christmas. She never experienced the cakes in the picture book, the large tree, or the presents.

Even the smiles drawn in the story were nowhere to be found in her home. To many people, that picture book was just like real life, but to Violette, it was a cruel pipe dream. She didn't feel strongly enough about it to hate it, but she disliked the book enough to not read it a second time. Just once was enough to burn the trauma into her memory. She could never tell Yulan that, however.

"That's why, you see... Here!"

With a heart-melting smile, Yulan stuck his hands out in front of her. He'd brought them so close to her face that she felt dazed, trying to focus. Something was twinkling on his palm.

"What?"

When she pulled back, she saw that it was a wreath, round but slightly crooked. The base was green, and it was decorated with lots of silver. It looked tiny in Yulan's hands.

"Um... What's this?" Violette asked. She tilted her head, unsure of what exactly was happening, so Yulan smiled even brighter.

"It's a Christmas present from me to you, Vio."

Violette's eyes went wide, and she was left stunned, unable to summon words. As she remained there, frozen, Yulan stood before her looking like a little kid who'd successfully pulled off his prank.

"Santa gives people Christmas presents, right? Well, then I can give you a present too."

There was no tree, no delicious cakes.

"Santa is supposed to bring you happiness," Yulan continued.

Santa did not come for her.

"So I want to be *your* Santa!"

Violette didn't like Christmas because it was a day when everyone was simultaneously happy—something she would never experience. There was no one to comfort her when she was tormented by the void inside her stockings.

Santa—or rather, parents who would lavish her with gifts—lay nowhere in sight.

"I made this. The ones sold at the stores are too big, and they're all in Christmas colors," Yulan told her.

"Oh."

"I thought these silver ribbons looked like your hair...but I ended up using so many that there weren't enough for the wrapping."

Violette held the small wreath in her hands, feeling bewildered. Her fingertips touched the stiff branches and caressed the smooth ribbons. It was in her hands now, but she remained in a trance, unable to accept that the gift was real. She didn't know how to react. What should she do? What was the right way to express herself? As she gazed at the thing sitting in the palms of her hands, she was swallowed up by the muddy stream of her jumbled thoughts. Nothing came out even when she opened her mouth. Only air drifted between the two of them.

Yulan misunderstood the reason for her confusion.

"Do you...not like it? Must be because I didn't do a good job making it."

"Oh, no! It's not that!" Violette cried in a panic.

The sorrow in Yulan's voice forced her to tear her gaze away from the wreath. Her bafflement meant nothing in the face of Yulan's discomfort.

Violette had no memories of Christmas. Until this very moment, she had never received a present. She had never happily eaten a cake. Never looked at her beautiful tree. Nothing. She had nothing.

Or she hadn't, until today. Until that moment.

"Thank you, Yulan... It's the first time I've had such a wonderful Christmas."

❧❀☙

"How nostalgic," Violette said to herself.

Violette's environment had changed rapidly after that, so she never got another chance to spend Christmas with Yulan. As they grew up, different problems would arise if she received a present from someone of the opposite sex.

The wreath had once fit in both her hands, but now she could easily hold it in one. It was the first Christmas present she had received since she was born, and the sole memory that she had of Christmas.

"I remember now. She hid it here for me."

As soon as she'd come home that day, she had run straight to Marin.

"Please hide it somewhere it can never be found," Violette had told her.

If her mother found it, she might throw it away. She might destroy it.

Bellerose had been vehemently against Violette getting involved with anyone else. She was only allowed to exist inside that room. Bellerose would call Violette to her room, shoo the servants away, and spend time alone with her daughter. That was her only reality; she rejected everything outside it.

If such a person had discovered that Violette treasured a gift from someone else, what would have happened? The answer was as clear as day.

"It was certainly safe here."

Marin had stashed the wreath in her closet, deep inside a drawer of loungewear. Even the owner of the closet didn't often venture this far. Violette hadn't known it was here until today.

"I should clean up."

Violette put away her Christmas memory along with all the gathered clothes. She was no longer the frightened girl from back then, but she still wanted to hide this precious treasure of hers. It was a memory that no one in this house had intruded upon. Her little secret that no one had soiled, no one had denied.

She didn't want anyone in this house to speak of it. To know of it. To touch it. The moment that someone did would be the moment that reality painted over her dream. This fragment of a meager wish would be scoffed at by anyone if even a word of it left her lips. But to Violette, it was proof that her dream came true; no matter how briefly.

In the far corner of a huge closet in the expansive mansion, Violette's only Christmas memory remained.

I Swear I Won't Bother You AGAIN!

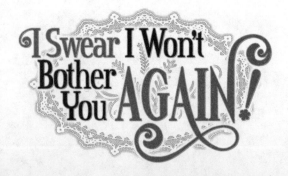

64 Pressure

$\mathbf{A}$s EXPECTED, THE SMOOTHER the study sessions went, the faster the actual exam period approached. By the time Violette had gotten used to walking to the salon, it was the day before exams.

Milania told Violette, "I think you'll do well considering your score here."

"You don't seem to have a problem with the memorization," Claudia observed.

They put together a mock exam for her based on their old ones and had just finished grading it now. Violette hadn't found any mistakes when she'd reviewed it herself, but the compliments given to her by older, adept students like these did a great job of reassuring her.

"Thank you very much."

"I'll give this back to you, so you should look over it a bit during your break," Milania said. He gave her the graded exam, and when she scanned the pages, everything was correct. While these questions weren't guaranteed to appear on tomorrow's exam, she still felt proud of her result.

"You two shouldn't have anything to worry about," Claudia said.

"Thank you so much!" Maryjune chirped.

"I truly appreciate it," Violette said.

"This'll be your first test, Maryjune," Claudia remarked. "But I think you'll get a good score."

"It's thanks to all of you!" Maryjune replied. "If I'd been by myself, I wouldn't have known what I should do. I would have ended up a total mess."

Through all their study sessions, Violette had grown accustomed to seeing the sight of Claudia with Maryjune as a pair. She would've been infuriated at every little detail of their partnership in the past, but this time, she hoped their relationship would stay smooth. Above all, what mattered most to her current self was the exam ahead.

I've taken this exam before, but I doubt I'll be able to ace it.

Her daily study sessions appeared to be a success. While she did remember taking it once, she hadn't memorized the questions. Her dark memories and experiences overshadowed all else, causing her recollection of the exam to fade. This time, she understood the lessons better, but that was it. She hadn't gained enough of an advantage to call it cheating.

She skimmed her answers and focused in on the parts she was feeling less confident about or had taken her a while to solve.

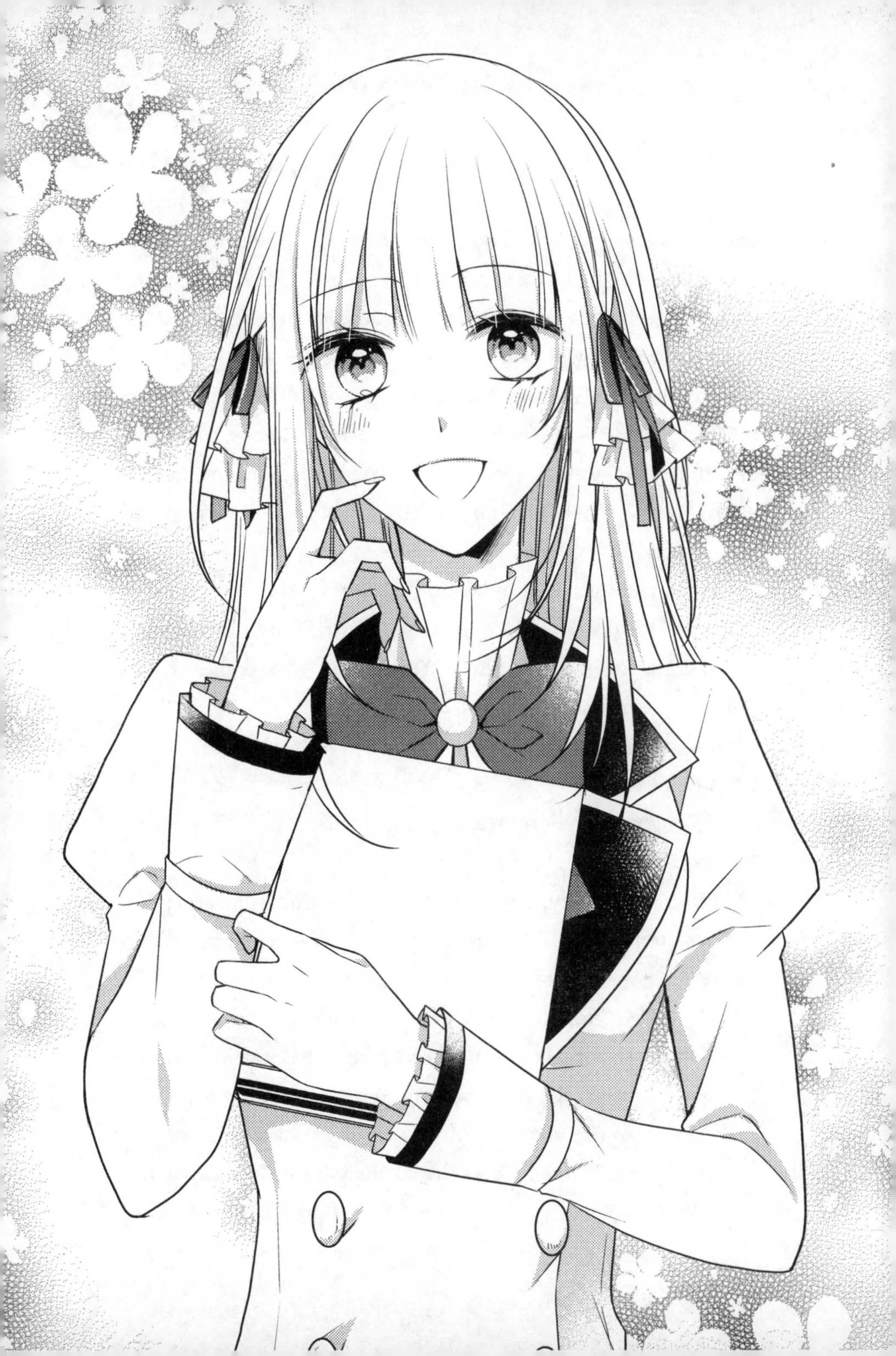

When Maryjune had taken on the exams all alone, she had easily shone as the top student. Given that she was even more prepared this time, she would no doubt pass with flying colors. As for the accompanying lecture from their father, Violette had already steeled herself. All the preparation in the world wouldn't help her here; she would merely do her best to ignore him like usual.

No, there was another reason that she couldn't botch the test this time: Yulan's care for her and Claudia's assistance. Maryjune might see their study sessions as a stroke of random luck or a novelty of her new life, but Violette knew how important and intentional those gifts were.

Yulan had been troubled and hesitant, but he'd still tried to help Violette. Claudia had reined in his distrust to assist a woman who'd done nothing but cause him grief. She had to do her utmost to repay them.

"You nervous?" Yulan asked her.

"Just a little."

"Thought so," he said with his usual soft smile. "Your face is looking a bit tense, y'know?"

He wasn't the type to fret over exams, but still, seeing her junior so much more relaxed than she was, Violette couldn't help but feel like she'd lost face.

She added, "I'm not nervous in a bad way, though."

It wasn't the usual tension, like a blade at her back or a grip on her heart. Instead, she felt a heavy sensation weighing her down, making it hard to move. She was practically crawling to bear the weight of it now, but that was what invigorated and drove her.

The heaviness came from the weight of everyone's efforts and expectations. This was surely what people called "pressure."

"I think...I have to do my best."

In her past life, Violette had never asked someone for help or wanted to repay their favor. Until now, she hadn't once thought about working hard for someone else's sake. And now, she didn't even know whether they were expecting anything from her in return, if there was some secret hurdle she had to get over.

Throughout her life, if she couldn't overcome the hurdles set before her, she'd be scolded and scorned. She was expected to always live up to someone else's expectations or to reach some secret, unattainable goal. And those expectations forced upon her were intolerable. Violette was never allowed to live for herself.

Her father always expected things from Violette for "someone else's sake." She wouldn't be praised if she succeeded, but she'd be verbally abused if she failed. It was like having her feet locked in place and being told to run to someone. She was ordered to move for another person, even if she had to crawl.

She'd wondered how that was different from being a slave. She didn't want that for herself. She hated the idea of being beholden to someone else's expectations forever. That thought had dominated her mind, forcing her to lose sight of herself. And when she committed her crime, she saw her punishment as being forced to atone to the most detestable "someone else" in the world.

Now, she could appreciate how foolish and dramatic her thinking had been.

People could not live solely for others, but they also couldn't live just for themselves. That idea was so simple, but she had never realized it before. But now, she *wanted* to repay Yulan—she wished to show results to pay back his kindness. The sentiment weighed on her, but she had never felt such comfortable pressure before.

"Uh, right. Good luck," Yulan said nonchalantly.

Violette didn't notice Yulan's dark expression as he averted his gaze, nor did she notice the shadow passing over his eyes. She only smiled at Yulan as she normally would, her eyes crinkling.

"You too. Let's both do our best."

She let out a giggle, simultaneously emanating an elder sister's dignity and pure innocence. As if it was the most natural thing in the world, Violette drew closer to Yulan. She had prepared a seat for Yulan in her world, unaware of how much salvation and joy it brought him.

"Yeah, let's."

"Did you get a perfect score on your questions too?" she asked.

"More or less. But old questions might not appear on this one, so I don't know if I'll do *that* well."

"Naturally."

"Sure would be easier if I did."

"Then there would be no point in having exams."

They were in their own world together. Not only were they childhood friends, but Yulan had embedded himself in Violette's consciousness little by little, and Violette had accepted him naturally.

Distracted by the comfortable atmosphere between them, Violette failed to notice something.

Yulan was the only one who caught sight of the golden eyes fixed on the two of them.

I Swear I Won't Bother You AGAIN!

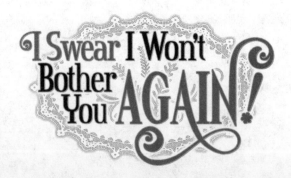

65 Admiration and Envy Are Alike

THEY REALLY ARE DIFFERENT, Claudia thought, suppressing a sigh.

He wasn't sure if the air around the two study groups did visibly vary in color or if it was just his imagination. It didn't matter, really. The world seen through his eyes would appear the same regardless.

Maryjune looked at Milania. "I'm grateful to you too, Lord Mila."

"Oh, I haven't done anything major," he replied.

"Sure you have! You showed me all sorts of helpful books!"

"You're the one who read and learned from them, Mademoiselle Maryjune."

The two of them wore smiles as they chatted in front of Claudia. Both Mila and Maryjune were naturally friendly, so they were comfortable with each other, like old friends. It was the same when she spoke with Claudia. They didn't need to read each other to figure out what to talk about.

Maryjune's purehearted disposition was absolutely radiant. Whether that was a blessing or a curse depended on the beholder, but Claudia personally thought she had a likable personality. In spite of that, something reined in his interest.

"You're surprisingly poor at humanities, Yulan."

"Am I? I had no idea."

"You take longer to answer these questions. When you were asked to analyze the text, you made little mistakes. You really didn't notice?"

"Oh... You're right."

"Well, you didn't make too many mistakes overall."

Claudia's ears picked up her voice. His eyes were drawn in her direction.

He just didn't understand why it had to be Violette. He felt restless whenever he talked to her. It wasn't possible for him to treat her in the same amicable way he did Maryjune. He was always on edge, unable to control his unsteady feet. This suffocating feeling made him want to avoid Violette, or at least ignore her.

Claudia didn't have to look at her. He didn't have to speak to her. If he didn't, he wouldn't have to endure this torment. And yet, he couldn't keep his eyes off her, couldn't stop himself from tuning out everyone else to hear her voice more clearly.

Up until recently, just seeing her had been unpleasant, and her unnaturally saccharine voice had grated on his ears. He'd wanted to forget all about her. He was supposed to *hate* her, but his gaze instinctively danced around her figure. He couldn't even think of looking away as he stared at her, burning her visage into his mind.

Until he saw a pair of golden eyes staring back.

Startled, Claudia let out a quiet noise of surprise. His whole body stiffened, frozen to the spot by the ice-cold glare directed his way. He felt ashamed of himself. It was much more uncomfortable for Yulan to have noticed than Violette. Yulan was Claudia's weakness; he was terrified of the younger boy.

Like a child awaiting a scolding, he felt his heart racing. The blood rushing through his head was deafening in his ears. Pinned by Yulan's stare, he racked his brain for an excuse to leave. However, his panic turned out to be unnecessary.

Yulan's gaze smoothly swung back to Violette, as if Claudia had never existed.

What?

"Hey, Vio. Once exams are over, do you want to go somewhere again?"

"Yes, of course. We can go wherever you'd like."

"Wherever I'd like?"

"I promised you I'd think of a reward, right? Though I think it'd be better if we chose together."

"Wow... Thanks, Vio!"

"I haven't done anything yet."

Violette smiled, so Yulan smiled back—so drenched in bliss he might melt. Everyone saw Yulan as soft and gentle, but Claudia knew that right now his heart was several times sweeter than usual. The prince thought that this scene looked perfectly complete—and almost blinding. Was it because he longed for the feelings she directed toward Yulan, the opposite of the ones he received?

This emotion he felt seeing that smile from Violette, the girl he despised...it was probably envy.

66 The Day I Crossed My Heart in Hell

YULAN COMPLETELY UNDERSTOOD what people meant when they called the eyes "the windows to the soul." Looking at someone was a sign of interest, so if it happened more often, that proved they were on your mind. Staring at someone helped engrave their image into your memory. Yulan knew for a fact that Claudia's heart was focused on Violette, though he didn't know if the accompanying feelings there were good or bad.

Still, he's easy to read.

Moments earlier, Yulan had noticed someone's gaze lingering on the two of them—or rather, just Violette—and was immediately able to identify the person in question. He was used to Claudia having that look on his face, as though he were about to say something, whenever they were near each other.

Had Yulan been the focus of that stare, he could easily ignore it. Annoyingly, however, Claudia's stare wasn't directed at him but squarely at Violette.

"I wonder if I'll have free time on the last day of exams?" Violette said.

"Maybe... Want to have an after-exam party, just us two?"

"Yeah. That sounds like fun."

Violette's smile dissolved Yulan's urge to click his tongue in frustration. It didn't matter whether Claudia's mind was still fixed on her, as long as Violette was happy. And, luckily, it seemed that she still wasn't aware of his gaze.

"We can go somewhere to eat lunch... Is there anything you want to do?" Violette asked.

"I... Well, nothing in particular comes to mind, hee hee."

Merely being with Violette fulfilled 90 percent of Yulan's desires. The remaining 10 percent was his desire for her love, but he knew it wasn't time for that yet. For the moment, at least, he was completely fulfilled.

Violette replied, "Think of where you'd like to go, then."

"You should pick—"

"No way. I want to repay you for all your hard work."

Despite her insistence, Yulan had already received his reward just by having Violette accompany him. As someone who normally didn't want much, he couldn't think of anything. Yulan's desires always revolved around Violette. Or, more precisely, Yulan's needs were inseparable from Violette's existence. If she weren't around, Yulan wouldn't even have the desire to breathe.

"Um..."

Yulan felt complicated. He didn't want to trouble Violette, and while he wanted to accept her reward, he had no idea what this "reward" could be. It should have been a welcome conundrum, but to him, it seemed even harder than taking exams.

"Let me think about it until then," he said, looking deeply vexed.

Truthfully, he couldn't think of anything, but he would come up with *some* kind of plan for her sake. That was groundless confidence, but he had conviction as he shunted the problem toward his future self. He figured he'd be fine.

"You don't have to if you don't want to."

"That's not it," he replied quickly. "Definitely not."

His denial was so vehement that Violette's uneasy face changed into one of surprise. As she sat there blinking, doe-eyed, she looked almost childlike to his eyes. He had to object, though—otherwise Violette would've misunderstood. She might've thought that she was being a nuisance or that he truly disliked the idea.

Yulan wondered how many people knew that Violette was hypersensitive to others' expressions and body language. She likely wasn't aware of it herself; in fact, Yulan thought she was a little bit dense when it came to this. But he simply pretended not to see her reaction and focused on keeping his expression calm. If he slacked off even a little, she would notice even the smallest of changes in his demeanor.

It wasn't that her inner antenna was good; on the contrary, it was broken and couldn't tell the important signals from the unimportant ones. She'd been born and raised in a world where she needed that hypervigilance to survive. Thus, it was best for him to be honest with her.

"I'm super excited about it, I swear. I just can't think of anything," Yulan admitted.

"I see. Sorry for dropping it on you all of a sudden."

"Nah. I just never realized how little I actually want."

"True, I rarely hear you say that you like something or that you want something."

"Yeah."

He wanted the girl in front of him so badly that he'd sacrifice himself in the process, but he knew he'd regret it if he struck too soon. Failure may be considered the mother of success by some people, but Yulan only had one chance to succeed at this. If he failed, he wouldn't be given another. And if he failed, it wouldn't just be him who was miserable but Violette too—and *that* he would never allow. A world that held a dark future for Violette was fundamentally *wrong*. Yulan would do anything to make her happy, even if it meant causing someone else to suffer.

Even if it caused someone else to suffer... Yes, that held true even if that person were Yulan himself.

He sat there for a moment in silent contemplation.

"Yulan?" Violette asked.

"Hey, Vio."

"Hm?"

Her large, round eyes took on a peculiar color as they reflected Yulan's visage. They sparkled so much that Yulan had once sworn they were jewels. Even though he had seen all sorts of real jewels since then, he still valued Violette's eyes above all else. They were two beautiful gems that grew even more so when she smiled. No matter when or where, Violette was the loveliest, most precious part of Yulan's world. He would let himself be cast down to the depths of hell, and he wouldn't even mind as long as Violette could smile happily.

Or so he'd thought.

"If I can't decide on something by then, let's come up with it together."

"Absolutely. I'll go wherever you'd like."

Was she really in love? Did she want him to love her?

The day she first fell in love, Yulan had wished for his goddess's happiness from his place in hell. And when that wish was crushed into pieces and blown away by the wind, he swore that he would never entrust Violette's happiness to anyone else ever again.

Her love was too precious to be wasted on a man who thought nothing of her, a *fool* who knew nothing of his goddess's nobility. That man had thrown Violette away because he didn't need her. It was far too late for him to covet her now. Claudia could curse his past self in the same depths of hell that Yulan had already experienced.

His eyes blurred with sheer hatred, with unspoken curses. Yulan chose to pretend that he hadn't noticed Claudia's gaze at all.

If she knew his feelings right now...

If Violette knew she was the object of Claudia's gaze, if she learned that she had charmed that man, if the day came when her wish to be loved was granted...

Who would Violette choose? Who could make her happy?

I Swear I Won't Bother You AGAIN!

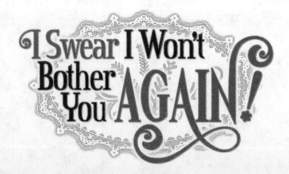

67   A Lifetime of White Flags

IN CONTRAST TO THE STUDY PERIOD, the exams only lasted three days, meaning that they passed by in a flash. It was a depressing time, with the one upside being that school ended earlier than usual. This would be the first time Violette could enjoy that.

Yulan stretched with a grunt. "Man, freedom feels great!"

"Yeah, we were in the thick of it for quite a while," said Violette, standing beside him.

Violette felt like a great weight had been lifted from her shoulders. She knew the relief was temporary, but she didn't want to dwell too much on the future anyway. She would happily relinquish herself to this moment.

"So, did you decide where you want to go?" she asked.

"More or less... I still haven't thought of anything that would make me say, 'I really want this!' so I was thinking we could wander around and look at a bunch of stuff." With an uneasy look, he asked, "Will you come with me?"

He lingered there, waiting for her like always. He'd been more direct than usual this time. Violette took it to mean that he'd grown up a little.

Truthfully, he was even more devoted to pleasing her than when he was younger, but she couldn't sense that.

"Of course."

When she brought a hand to her mouth to stifle her giggles, she looked more at ease than usual. Yulan couldn't tell whether she lacked any sorrow to speak of or if she was indulging in escapism, but she was enjoying herself either way. Yulan resolved to act with care; stepping on her toes would spoil his plans for today. If Violette was going to join him in his selfish endeavor, Yulan had a responsibility to devote his body and soul to please her. In the end, he could only try to preserve Violette's present smile.

"The binder I've been using is wearing out, so I was thinking about going to get it fixed," Yulan said.

"Aah. Now that you mention it, it *does* look a bit frayed in places."

"I've been using it since middle school."

Yulan stowed his papers and such in a leather binder with his initials branded on its caramel-colored surface. She recalled hearing that his parents had bought it for him to celebrate his enrollment into the academy. Yulan generally took care of his belongings, and he'd continued to use this binder even after it started falling apart out of consideration for his parents. But carrying it around in this state made him come off as unrefined or even neglectful.

He'd apparently decided that it was time for a change. He could have had it repaired, mended, or even fixed. Doing so would make it a firm fixture of Yulan's personality that he cared for his belongings. If anything, he should have chosen something that would last a lifetime from the outset; whether through extending its life span as much as possible through maintenance, or better, by using it long enough for it to adapt to him.

Violette sympathized with his way of thinking. While he was giving it due attention now, he'd only done so after it had noticeably deteriorated. He hadn't yet reached a point where he regularly saw to his possessions. Still, this way was much better than leaving it until it broke. She thought it was very like him, when it came right down to it.

"When I thought about it," Yulan continued, "I realized I've got to fix or replenish a bunch of things, like the ink for my pens... but I don't need anything new."

"I see. After all those study sessions, you must've exhausted most of your supplies."

"None of them were completely done for, though. Today, I'll probably be just going around for repairs."

"That should still be fun, right?"

"If you think so, then sure."

Once they settled on a plan, they set off. Violette tagged along as Yulan stopped by the first shop, entrusting his bag to the repairman. They would come back to pick it up later on. He then bought ink at a second store, and he had his pens fixed at a third.

After this bit of store-hopping, Yulan said, "I think that's all."

"It was less than I thought," Violette told him.

"Really? Well, I didn't have much on me anyway."

As it was the final day of exams, Yulan's bag—usually chock-full of textbooks—had been nearly empty. He'd only carried the items he wanted repaired, but aside from those, he had just his wallet and pencil case.

"How are we on time, Vio?"

"Huh?" Violette glanced at the pocket watch tucked inside her bag. "Uh, it might still be too early."

The repairman wouldn't be finished with Yulan's binder yet. Even if they stopped by now, they would still have to wait.

"Right... Wanna go take a break somewhere?" Yulan suggested.

Quite some time had passed since their lunch at noon, and all that walking had made them hungry. They were going to have dinner back at their own homes, but they could at least get tea or pick up some sweets. Yulan's eyes wandered as they searched for the right place. There were a lot of artisan shops here, so only a few places served food and drinks. The area didn't see much foot traffic either, so a café would have a hard time getting business.

Still, there weren't just cafés but plenty of restaurants lining the district a little farther away. If they went all the way there and back, however, they would barely have enough time to relax. Yulan racked his brain for a place where Violette could relax and enjoy some delicious sweets and tea. He brought a finger to his chin in contemplation.

It was then that Violette noticed something about him.

"Hey, Yulan. What happened to your watch?"

She had seen Yulan's wrist peek out of his sleeve. A simple wristwatch had adorned it only yesterday, but today, it was bare.

"Huh?" He gave her a puzzled look, then followed her gaze. "Oh, I lost it."

His wrist felt lighter than normal, but because it became easier to move, he had completely forgotten. If it had been anyone else, Violette would've been worried, but his indifference exasperated her.

"Isn't that the fourth one now?" she asked him.

"Unfortunately, no. It's the sixth."

"That's even worse."

"I knooow." He sulked, puffing out his cheeks like he had as a child. "But I'm not good with wristwatches."

While Yulan took care of his other belongings, he habitually took off his wristwatches and forgot where he left them. He and Violette used to go searching for them, but he never changed regardless of how many times she reprimanded him. She'd pretty much given up. Yulan now bought only cheap wristwatches, in a mild act of defiance.

"No matter which one I get, they all feel uncomfortably tight on my wrist. It's hard to move, and even when the size is right, it feels like it's constricting me."

"I get that, but won't you have a hard time without one?"

"Not at school. I guess it's a little annoying elsewhere, though."

"Thought so."

The classrooms in the academy were equipped with clocks and ringing bells, so Yulan never had a problem. Still, having a sense of time was important, and it would be better for him to use his own method in that regard. Time was money, and its importance was enough to sway anyone's trust.

"I wonder if watches feel tight on you because of your thick wrists," Violette said.

Wristwatches for women were designed to feel like bracelets, but the ones for men had bands mostly made of leather or metal and fit snugly on the wrist. This was especially true given the thickness of Yulan's wrists in relation to his size. His wrists, twice as broad as Violette's, were bony; if the band was too loose, the watch would smack against the bone and hurt him.

"I'm also not a fan of wristwatches... Oh." Violette appeared to have come to her own conclusions about something. "Right, there's that."

"Vio? What's the matter?"

Yulan waved his hand in front of her while she nodded to herself, deep in thought, but this attempt to obstruct her line of sight was fruitless. Just as Yulan was about to devote himself to watching over her, Violette raised her face and stared straight at him.

"Uh, Vio?"

"Are you hungry? Or maybe tired?"

He faltered. "No, I'm all right, but..."

"Then I know just the thing."

"Huh? What're you—?!"

Violette grabbed Yulan by the wrist. Her hand wasn't large enough to fully wrap around it, but the sensation of her soft palm was present enough. As she charged ahead, he did his best to match her stride. Her steps, however swift, moved her at Yulan's walking pace. Objectively speaking, Violette was weaker and slower than Yulan overall. And yet, the young Yulan had thought that this person was an immaculate guardian. She protected him.

The first time he'd felt the urge to protect *her* was when he finally realized how small and soft she really was. Her hands were so small, they couldn't even hold on to his wrist. And yet, Yulan would never be a match for her. He would lose to just one of her fingers, or even the tip of her fingernail. He had absolutely no power to resist her.

"Is there somewhere you want to go?" he asked her.

He didn't know where they were heading or what they were going to do. But no matter where she went, he would follow. She didn't need to hold him; he would've done so even if she didn't tell him to. Still, there was no need for him to say anything and ruin this blessed experience.

Violette looked back at him, smiling brightly.

"We're going to buy your reward, Yulan."

I Swear I Won't Bother You AGAIN!

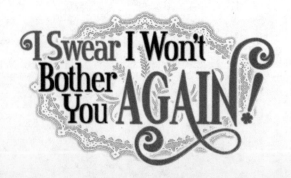

68 Protective Sacrifice

VIOLETTE LED YULAN to a watch store. It was nearby, so they could go pick up his fixed-up binder once they finished here. They no longer had time for a break, but Yulan wasn't tired in the first place. Since Violette had prioritized this new plan, he had no intention to object. He also didn't need to ask why they'd come.

"I bought my own watch here. They have all kinds, not just wristwatches. Plenty of designs too," Violette explained.

"Oh, so you've been here before."

"Of course I...haven't. It's also my first time, actually. Marin was the one who chose my watch for me."

"Aah, I see."

Violette couldn't handle accessories well either; the wristwatches she owned hadn't been selected with her tastes in mind. They were all her father's old ones or custom orders of the exact same designs. The overwhelming majority were designed for men, so naturally, they'd often slipped off Violette's thin wrist.

Until Marin purchased her current pocket watch, Violette

had used wristwatches that suited her taste. They were awfully simple in design with a faux-leather strap attached to the case, but they were far better than the rest. She still hadn't gotten used to the feeling of having her wrist constricted and had consequently worn them until she lost them too many times to count, so Marin had found her the one she used now.

"With this, you can attach it to your bag or put it in your pocket, right?" Violette said.

She scanned the dials lined up side by side, searching for one that would fit Yulan. While she'd left the matter of her own watch to Marin, she was excited about choosing Yulan's. When things were chosen for her, she merely judged whether they suited her afterward, but the responsibility of picking out one that Yulan would like made everything fun. She was likely enjoying it *because* she was doing it for him. She had a good idea of his preferences, so if she chose something weird, he'd smile rather than criticize her.

"Your hands are pretty large, so a small one would be a pain to use."

"Exactly... But I'll treasure whatever you choose."

"That's not why I brought it up..."

Violette had originally planned to take the lead regardless, but judging by how Yulan grinned and trailed behind her, he appeared to be happy enough to entrust her with the decision. The watch no longer held his attention. All he could see now was his dear, troubled Violette.

"You'll be using it, so you have to make sure it's comfortable," she insisted, picking up one that had caught her eye.

Yulan cared little about design, so functionality was more important. Something sturdy that could sit in his hand would be good.

Hmm...

The larger watches fit perfectly in her palm, but they were probably too small for Yulan. If they were too inconspicuous, they would end up sharing the same fate as his other wristwatches: forgotten and neglected. Yulan's trend of losing his wristwatches probably stemmed from the fact that he'd never worn one growing up.

Violette wanted him to use her gift for as long as possible. She wanted him to like it. In truth, her worry was completely unnecessary, but she wasn't privy to Yulan's inner thoughts.

"If it's going to fit in my hand, it'll need to be pretty big, don't you think?" Yulan asked with a wave, as though to demonstrate its relative size.

"Well...that's true."

His hand was large enough to completely cover her face, though that was a given based on his height. If she handed over the pocket watch, which nicely fit in the palm of her hand, it would be like giving Yulan a toy.

"As long as I can easily move it in and out of my pocket, then that's fine. It'll be a bother if it's too large."

He said it like it was someone else's problem. She wondered if he realized that he'd be using it...or if he knew and was leaving everything up to her anyway. If it was the latter, then that was rather nasty of him. Should she choose an eccentric or cumbersome one,

Yulan would still see it as Violette choosing the best brand for him, and there would be nothing to worry about. Violette, however, saw this opportunity to gift Yulan something he had lost, so she wanted *some* kind of hint. She'd considered choosing it herself, but she truly wanted him to be happy with the watch he received.

She puffed out her cheeks and stared up at Yulan, whose smile remained steadfast. Faster than Yulan could say anything about her little pout, she wrapped both hands around his arm and tugged him closer.

"If you find something you like, make sure to let me know."

Yulan was speechless.

Her surprise attack brought her eyes closer to him, exposing Yulan's dazed face. He blinked profusely, but he was far from uncomfortable. Only a simple chuckle escaped his lips, like he was tolerating a child's prank.

"Okay, okay. Then let's choose one together."

"But you're the one who'll be using it, y'know?"

Although it was under the pretense of a reward, he didn't have to obediently accept whatever she chose. He was right there with her, so he might as well offer his opinion. He would enjoy picking one out alongside her too.

"How's yours?" Yulan asked.

"Mine? I..." Violette said.

Violette thought it would be faster to show him, so she retrieved her pocket watch from inside her bag. Its type was known as a half-hunter or a demi-hunter. The center of the cover was shaped like a doughnut and inlaid with glass. The inside was silver with a simple construction, and the cyan jewel at the axis of the clock hands shone brilliantly.

Yulan thought Marin had chosen something that really suited Violette, but looking at it now, he was reminded of Marin herself.

"She told me it's a charm," Violette said. "You know, to keep me safe."

"Ah, I get it now."

The jewel was the color of a serene ocean, so it was most likely aquamarine. Had Marin chosen it because of the jewel's symbolism or because her name was nestled in the jewel's? It was most likely a bit of both. Yulan didn't know much about Marin, but he knew for a fact that she treasured Violette. As long as she fulfilled that qualification, he didn't care about anything else. Above all, Marin was someone whom Violette trusted from the bottom of her heart; he didn't want to say or do anything that aroused Violette's suspicion or caused her to think badly of him.

So he said, "Well, good for you."

"Yeah."

Her delightful smile as she gingerly held the pocket watch conveyed how precious it was to her. She had scant few opportunities to receive things from others, let alone gifts chosen with her in mind. When she thought about it, the first present she had ever received as "Violette" had been from Yulan. She had gotten many gifts as a child—including presents for Christmas and her birthday—but none of them had been given to her because she was Violette.

"I would've liked to get matching ones, but not anymore."

"Huh? Oh, right, it'll probably be too small for you."

"That too, but... Yeah, I'll choose something else."

Violette looked puzzled.

Her pocket watch made him think of Marin, but it certainly matched Violette's tastes. She normally didn't like excessive ornamentation. Its size and delicate design gave the impression that it was for women, but a man could use it without attracting curious glances. Yulan wasn't sensitive enough to care about the impressions of others, anyway. He would have normally jumped right in to getting a matching pair, and Violette would've surely agreed with a smile.

But this watch, this present, was something Marin had chosen for Violette. It wasn't something he should imitate lightly. He had to observe certain etiquette when it came to dealing with a fellow devotee like Marin. If Yulan were in Marin's shoes, it would be uncomfortable to know that Yulan chose a present emphasizing the happiness she'd granted to Violette. Though they shared the same feelings toward Violette, Yulan felt he should stick to this unspoken rule.

"There are a lot that would fit you, but none of them feel quite right."

"I'll be happy with anything you choose."

"Oh, stop saying stuff like that. Wouldn't it be better if it suited you?"

As Yulan looked at Violette's troubled profile, he could sense that his mouth had softened into a smile. He rarely displayed feelings of like or dislike to begin with, so few people actually understood his preferences. In that sense, Violette didn't fully grasp Yulan's true nature either, but she did know a few of his likes and dislikes. That was enough to understand his values.

Her head was filled with thoughts of Yulan at this moment. The fact that she was thinking only of him was enough to fill Yulan's heart with so much joy, he feared it might rupture. He desperately wished that time would stop.

"Yulan, are you listening?"

"I'm listeniiing."

"Jeez, you only say that when you're *not* listening. Are there any here you like?"

"Hm. I mentioned wanting one that's easy to wear, so if I have to choose based on looks…" He trailed off, unable to complete the thought.

Violette's pouting face clouded with concern. Alas, it meant their merry trip had come to an end. Delaying any further would only worry her. No matter how much he might want time to stop, he knew that it wouldn't. *What an ironic thing to wish for,* Yulan thought to himself, *in a store that sells time itself.*

He didn't know how long they'd been here, but he needed to go pick up his binder. They couldn't loiter for much longer here. He should give her a reason to leave this store without buying anything, in that case. If he explained that he couldn't pick a watch, Violette would probably accept it, and he could use this as an excuse to invite her out again another day.

No matter how calculated of a move this was, Violette was sure to go along with it as long as he retained the image of a sweet younger brother. He announced that they would leave for the day, making full use of that side of her. Or at least, that was what he intended to do.

Her attention suddenly fixed elsewhere, Violette uttered a soft, "Oh."

"What is it, Vio?"

Violette took two or three steps, as if drawn in by the sight. She stopped in front of a shelf they hadn't looked at yet, knelt down, and stared at one of the pocket watches. Her searching eyes sparkled in delight, as if they'd landed on something certain.

"Thought so."

"Something wrong?" Yulan asked.

"Look. It's my watch."

"Hm?"

Yulan wondered what she meant by that, but her smile was so mischievous that he doubted she would explain. Puzzled, he followed her pointing finger...and everything slid into place instantly.

It was a hunter-case pocket watch. Flowers with strange, extraordinarily large petals clustered to fill its entire cover. The inset jewels, each a diluted purple color, formed a beautiful flower bed.

"Huh... It really is your watch, Vio."

The watch was adorned with violets, so it was no wonder that one might associate it with her like that. Incidentally, it hadn't been her parents who named her Violette but her maternal grandfather. She'd never asked for the reason behind it. Seeing a violet in the wild and reconciling it with her own name felt rather pleasant.

"I'm sorry for saying that out of nowhere. When I saw it, I just…"

"No worries."

Violette's gaze had fallen on it by happenstance, but she was supposed to be looking for a gift for Yulan. She might have bought this one for herself, but Marin had already gifted her with a watch; she didn't need another one. She also doubted Yulan would want to wear it. Between the pale coloring and the subtle violet pattern, the flowerbed design beneath the cover was rather subtle. It was an elegant piece with a graceful beauty and charm, but it looked too delicate for a man. Above all, something so fragile didn't suit Yulan. Violette automatically discounted it as a worthy gift.

"Hey, Vio. I want this one."

Before she could turn around, Yulan picked up the violet pocket watch. It had a long chain, perhaps so you could wear it around your neck if you liked, and it jangled when the metal parts bumped into each other. He brought it up to eye level to stare at it with a delighted expression. His childlike eyes were bright, like sunlight filtered through glass marbles. The air around him grew somewhat sweeter.

"Um…"

"This'll be my reward," he said firmly.

He understood, without a doubt, what she was thinking, but he refused to yield. He found something that would connect him to Violette. That alone made it special. He wouldn't dare hand it

I SWEAR I WON'T BOTHER YOU AGAIN!

over to anyone else. His desire bordered on monopoly, but it was nevertheless a deep and weighty emotion.

"I'll make this into a charm for myself."

"I wonder if it comes with any special powers?" Violette mused.

"Of course it does. I can tell for a fact that I won't ever lose or forget about it."

"Does that count?"

Violette sighed in resignation. Yulan sounded like an adoring younger brother, so she indulged him with her usual sisterly smile. The reality behind his words wasn't quite so charming, but Violette didn't have to know about that. She could see and believe what she wanted; it was Yulan's mission and raison d'être to make that happen.

"If you like it, then that'll be the one."

"Yeah, thanks!"

Yulan would lie in wait, biding his time. He prepared for every possible situation. Slowly, meticulously, he constructed the castle of her happiness, a fortress where no one could hurt her. His goal was to build a paradise for her and her alone.

It was fine that Violette didn't know of his real aims. She could remain unaware until the day of reckoning came. The idea of having Violette wait in the Vahan household in the meantime was revolting enough to make him sick, but if he rushed and failed, all his efforts would go down the drain.

He would do anything, use anyone, so she could follow her dreams without anguish or intervention. Yulan would offer up everything at his disposal, be it himself or other people. He would sacrifice his happiness for Violette's sake. He'd do so even if, by chance, his thoughts didn't reach her and his love ran amok. Even if his thoughts withered without bearing fruit. It mattered not.

The only thing he would never, ever do was hurt her.

I Swear I Won't Bother You AGAIN!

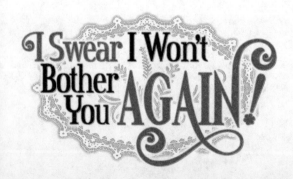

69 | The Cost of Giving Up

SURPRISINGLY, VIOLETTE DIDN'T HAVE an official curfew. That didn't mean she had plenty of freedom; in fact, it stemmed from a much larger problem. Maryjune and her stepmother were the arbiters of Violette's curfew, rather than the girl herself or her father. If either of them was worried about Violette, her curfew became a huge issue; if neither one was, she was free to stay out all night long. They might talk badly of her for such tardiness, but they wouldn't care a lick about her safety. Violette was bitterly aware that none of them held a genuine grain of concern for her. Her heart had already withered so much that such a thought did not wound her.

She no longer experienced surges of emotion or willpower. Even if she was dissatisfied, she had reached the point of letting everything go in one ear and out the other. Whatever she felt, consequences always followed. It was easier to resign herself to being their punching bag. It was hardly healthy to accept such a lot in life, but she never believed a healthy life in this house was possible to begin with.

"I was nervous, but I think I did my very best!" Maryjune said.

"There's my girl. It was your first test, so I'm sure you were quite nervous," Auld replied.

Violette had forced herself to become a machine again today, relegating the three smiling people around her to the background. Now she was an automaton unable to move anything but her hands and mouth. Whether her taste buds functioned depended on the day; they were like a roulette that operated outside her control. There were times when she thought the food was delicious, but whenever she tried to blot out her emotions the same food would turn into a tasteless mass of nutrients without fail.

It was truly regrettable, especially considering it had been made to her tastes. As delicious as the meals she ate in her room were, their flavor was influenced by the people around her. She ignored the nauseating discomfort nevertheless and forced her stomach to digest the food if only because the servants had made it for her. She did not savor the bland texture on her tongue, nor the sensation of it going down her throat.

At the same time, she wondered what would happen to her after the results of their exams came out. The mere thought of it made her feel like the weight deep in her gut had multiplied.

The exam results were temporarily posted in the hallway of the academy. Maryjune was in a different grade, so Violette didn't know how she'd done. If things went the same way as last time, Maryjune would dominate first place. Her half sister had easily obtained the top spot even without Violette's aid. Now that the girl had had an easier time, there was no need to bother checking.

I'm in fourth place, huh?

What place had she achieved last time? Violette could no longer recall, but it undoubtedly was somewhere in the upper range. Most people valued such high grades. Her father, on the other hand, had condemned her for placing lower than her younger sister. Violette still would've been scolded had she placed higher—just a bit less. Violette's father was never going to praise her. It didn't just lie outside the realm of possibility; it was fate.

To begin with, Violette was just an embarrassing older sister who couldn't get first place over Maryjune. But if, hypothetically speaking, Violette studied in a frenzy and took first place, she would hear no praise nor lecture for her pains. That would be the end of it. It was terribly unfair. Violette was considered as an intruder, all by herself. The other three believed themselves to be the ideal family.

Well, I'm used to it now.

Violette had long since given up. All she could do was let out a tired sigh. No anger welled up within her; she had already failed once, so she knew it would be a waste of energy.

"I wonder how Yulan did," Violette said to herself.

The lack of concern, expectations, and many other things besides that Violette felt for her half sister meant she had little to no interest in her results.

Yulan was another story. He was similar to Maryjune in that people flocked to him and he had a lot of practical skills. He wasn't an oblivious genius like Maryjune, though—he was aware of his own abilities. Still, it didn't change the fact that he was outstanding.

Violette couldn't feel at ease not knowing because she still saw Yulan as somewhat of a child. She wasn't *worried* about him per se, but concern still wormed its way into her heart. The small boy who used to hide behind her back had matured into a splendid young man. To Violette, however, he was still her adorable friend, practically her younger brother, and more precious to her than her own family. While he was only a year younger, she couldn't help but act like his older sister.

She bitterly smiled at her own feelings, resembling an overprotective mother.

"He worked hard, and I'm sure he got a good grade, but..." She couldn't imagine how well he might've done.

It occurred to her that her past self had never asked about Yulan's exam results even once. She hadn't been composed enough to do so. Not only had Maryjune ground her pride into dust, but her father had scorned and berated her. Accustomed to being ignored, she found it painfully ironic that he had demanded she put effort into her studies while snubbing the efforts she'd made. It must have made some sort of sense in Auld's mind. Violette was amazed that she had survived a whole year after fighting back. Well, a year's worth of built-up resentment had finally erupted, resulting in her being thrown in prison.

With all this plaguing her mind, past-Violette couldn't afford to be concerned about Yulan. Rather, she was the one who had been handled with care, the one who worried others. She may have given up on everything, but if the result was her now having the leeway to think about Yulan, then it was a decent payoff.

Oh, I have to thank those two later.

Thanks to Claudia and Milania, Violette had done better than she would have had she studied alone. She intended to thank Yulan again for setting everything up, but she needed to include those two for supervising Maryjune's studies as well. She had no intention of acting on her half sister's behalf; she just didn't expect that Maryjune would thank them properly. She had manners, but her worldview was still that of a commoner. Her mindset had seemingly improved, but Violette couldn't allow her to make any kind of misstep when the prince was involved.

If Maryjune *did* make a mess, Violette would be the one to suffer. The consequences wouldn't come from Claudia or the others but from their love-blind father. In order to protect Maryjune, he might force Violette to take the responsibility for her ignorance.

I'll ask Marin to prepare something for them.

Violette didn't know the gentlemen's tastes, so she thought something universally liked would be best. Sweets were probably a safe bet. She'd try asking their head chef. Claudia and the others had seemed to enjoy the chef's favorite tea leaves, so she could interrogate him about other rare ingredients after dinner.

First, though, she must endure her father's unreasonable lecture. It dawned on her that the reason she no longer felt anger at this indignation wasn't because of growth but rather regression, so she did her best to stop thinking about it.

•

70 Worth as Much as Carbon Dioxide

THE HAPPY, PAPIER-MÂCHÉ FAMILY CIRCLE was as suffocating as always. Accustomed to it as Violette was, she still felt tormented in this space. All she'd done was endure its difficulty and establish a way to tolerate it. Today was at least 30 percent more agonizing than usual. There was a crushing pain in her chest, and even the act of chewing and swallowing was a struggle. The discomfort was similar to heartburn.

"Are you listening, Violette?" came Auld's voice.

"Yes."

Any attempts to escape her reality were foiled immediately. Despite ignoring Violette most of the time, Auld was reprehensibly sharp at times like this. She needn't sugarcoat things at this stage—this tendency of his was one of the most unbearable things for her to put up with. He'd been prodding her for such responses for some time now, so she hoped he'd think she was sincere in offering these curt replies. It was a far better compromise than purposely ignoring him, as she had done before.

In the past, she would bite back at a single word. When three times the scolding turned into five times, an uncontrollable quarrel would break out. To the Violette of this time, raising that much trouble was nothing more than a waste of energy.

"Good grief... You should follow Mary's example. You're supposed to be the older sister, yet you're flagging behind her. Have you no shame?"

"I apologize," Violette said mechanically.

If her emotionless stock response would satisfy him, she didn't mind if it came at the cost of her self-respect. She had been cruelly beaten numerous times already, so it was quite possible she might shatter. Snapping here might even strip her of all her emotions. The despair that came next would be comfortable, in a way. She may wish to die were she to remain in that state for too long, but hopefully she could recover before it reached that point.

After all, she had always been fine before. Numerous times since then, she had been broken, crushed, and sometimes even snuffed out her own sense of self. Putting her emotional heart to death didn't stop the physical organ from functioning. It would take time, and treatment, and no small amount of pain, but after that she would be able to use it once again.

"Father, you can't say it like that!" Maryjune whined.

The sight of Maryjune puffing out her cheeks must have made an impact on some people. To their father, she must have looked just like a kitten playfully trailing after him. And yet, this gesture had enough power to end his lecturing. For someone who completely overlooked all the blood draining from Violette's face, he sure took a complete turn after this one comment from Maryjune. A brisk change of attitude, indeed. Now that it had come to this, Violette may as well have been the air around the two of them. Not the oxygen they breathed in but the unnecessary carbon dioxide they exhaled.

In place of the weight lifting from her shoulders, she felt the burden on her stomach increase—a common symptom of stress. If someone would kindly open up a hole in reality for her, Violette would be only too happy to climb into it and live there forever without taking any further part in this farce...but no, Maryjune was bound to worry and fuss about her. That would inevitably lead to complaints and then a lecture on comporting herself with more grace. If Violette were the sort to change her whole sense of self after being pushed to the limit, then Bellerose's plans for her would have succeeded.

"It must have been hard since it was your first test," Auld told Maryjune.

"I was super nervous, but it was fun!"

Maryjune's glittering smile was absolutely cherubic, and its innocence wounded Violette. To describe something that had made Violette distraught as "fun" was just the girl's disposition at work. Geniuses could be so inadvertently cruel... No, it hurt specifically because it was coming from Maryjune.

Marin, standing behind Violette, felt something beyond simple anger and dismay. The daughter who wholly believed in her father's love was framing the irrational reprimand he'd given her older sister as an act of love too. The blame really lay with her parents, but Marin couldn't help being disgusted by this daydreaming princess who was incapable of seeing things as they really were. Maryjune was free to believe that humans were inherently good or value their goodwill. If that attitude served as a blindfold that hid Violette's injuries, though, Marin could only take it as the gravest of sins.

If only Marin had Violette's permission! No, she hardly needed permission. She was ready to beat the three of them until she lost sensation in her fists. She only abstained from it because she knew that even that wouldn't help them to understand their own foolishness. Marin had lost track of how many days she wished for them to drop dead.

Meanwhile, Auld praised his little girl. "You did your best. You are our pride and joy."

"Thank you, Father. All of this is thanks to Violette!"

"Ghk!"

Just as Violette clamped her lips around her fork, a strange sound echoed deep in her ears. She somehow managed to stop herself from choking, but she was still quite shocked. When she looked up, she made eye contact with the grinning Maryjune. Violette was reminded how little they resembled each other as sisters. Violette couldn't smile that carefreely, nor could she imagine *wanting* to smile in such a situation.

"I was only able to get such a good grade because of the study sessions with Violette and everyone else!"

"Well... That's good," Violette said.

"Yeah!"

If Violette carelessly prolonged the conversation, the sharpness in her father's gaze would increase. She could easily imagine the future lecture she would get for carrying on a conversation that did not benefit Maryjune. When Violette brought it to a halt, Maryjune thankfully shifted her attention toward her parents.

Violette lowered her gaze to her meal, ready to resume eating. That was when she heard something even more surprising.

"Still, Yulan is really smart. He's at the top of the first-years!"

"Huh?" Violette blurted.

"I worked hard, but I couldn't compare to him."

Caught off guard by the sudden reveal, Violette couldn't bring herself to respond.

Yulan got first place?

She knew that Yulan was excellent, but she had never heard of him ever taking first place before. Before time rewound, the one who'd been top of the grade was Maryjune. Violette was aware that her dark history was useless. No matter how much she tried to lie low, the world changed as if to remind her she would not get away with it. Her father was the most extreme case of this; an antithesis to the adage that there was no smoke without fire, as Violette found herself choking to death on soot even as she dodged flame after flame. She never had any intention of objecting to this altered future, but she couldn't believe this was the result.

It's the result of our combined efforts, huh?

While the group study sessions and the time she'd spent with Claudia hadn't been very enjoyable for Yulan, they had

progressed far beyond what they could have done by themselves...
Yulan's emotional aims aside, of course.

I see. That's wonderful.

Violette feigned indifference as she suppressed the smile that
threatened to break out on her face. Flowers fluttered in her heart,
but she wondered what kind of backlash she'd face if her father
noticed. She would naturally be rebuked if she praised someone
who had beaten Maryjune.

"Right," Violette murmured, as if disinterested.

Being too blunt would incur her father's displeasure. She
needed to keep that in mind, lest her joy leak out. Luckily,
Maryjune hadn't noticed and continued chatting away, so
Violette managed to slip into the background once more. As
Maryjune's voice went in one ear and out the other, Violette's
mind drifted elsewhere. She was as delighted as though it were
her own achievement.

Although she would have liked to hear it from him first, she
thought she should plan a celebration for him. Yulan would no
doubt come rushing over as soon as he could to receive her praise,
but she might get a head start and compliment him first. Her
frozen heart slowly melted, growing warm again. It felt as if Yulan
had given her the power to persevere.

Maryjune said, "Now that I have the chance, I want to get
closer to Yulan!"

These words were supposed to pass through Violette's ears
like the rest, but instead, they grew heavy and took root deep
inside her mind.

71 Disappointment

Violette's mind was the source of her five senses: her second heart, the organ high above the nerves of her body. Nestled deep within was a soft, delicate feeling, more precious to her than any other—and right now, she could acutely sense it being crushed to bits.

She didn't exactly feel pain. Only at a time like this did the sense of intimidation she always felt from her father quiet down. This monotonous lack of emotion weighed on Violette's shoulders, and she was unable to register that feeling as good or bad. Her chest felt tight, and a cold sweat dripped down her back. She had been acting as a bystander this whole time, but now she could no longer remain objective.

Was this unease what people referred to as fear? She wondered what was making her afraid, if it was.

"We're in different classes, but we're still the same grade," Maryjune went on. "If he's your friend, I want to try talking to him about all kinds of things!"

"O-oh..."

Even though Violette was sitting, the ground felt unstable under her feet. She even imagined the floor dropping out from underneath her. She couldn't go anywhere. She couldn't escape. She had been driven into a corner by that innocent, smiling face directly in front of her.

It was hard to breathe. Her lungs weren't working properly. She couldn't even swallow her saliva as her esophagus tightened. She felt dizzy, and everything in her view distorted. She knew her current state was abnormal, but why was she feeling this scared now?

Wh-why is this happening?

When Violette thought about Maryjune's personality, the statement seemed very like her. The girl had a benevolent, magnanimous heart, so she wanted to fill it with everything she could. Maryjune had spoken to Yulan numerous times already, in fact, although their personalities apparently didn't match. He saw her as nothing more than Violette's younger sister.

Violette already knew that things would be different this time. Once Claudia had apologized to her, she steeled herself so that she wouldn't be surprised by any further changes. In actuality, she wasn't shocked at this development. If anything, she felt some comfort that it lay within the realm of her expectations. There was no cause for surprise nor panic...but for some reason she couldn't brush away the dread looming over her.

"That reminds me," Maryjune began, changing the subject. "Lately, I've been able to chat with my classmates more often."

For better or worse, the girl had moved on, jabbering excitedly to her parents. Violette looked at her from afar. Maryjune wore a brilliant smile as she chatted about today's mundane events, while her parents drank it all in.

But to the current Violette, her own uncontrollable thoughts were far more important than that faraway world. The fear that should have passed through her continued to lurk inside her mind.

⋰⋰⋰⋱⋱⋱

"Lady Violette..."

"I'm sorry, Marin. I'm...going to rest for a little."

"As you wish. If you need anything, please let me know."

"Thanks."

After Marin left, the only sound in the room was Violette's unsteady breathing. The noise grated on her ears, while the exaggerated thumping of her heart felt uncomfortable. Fear washed over her in wave after countless wave. The figure reflected in her dresser mirror looked faint. Her normally fair skin had a terrible pallor, drained of all its color. On closer inspection, her thin lips were trembling; her forehead glistened with moist sweat.

She was terrified. Something had scared her to the core. The scene had already ended, but it continued to entwine inescapably around her.

Yulan...with that girl!

Violette pictured Maryjune smiling lovingly next to Yulan. Such an amiable pair looked completely natural standing together. They would surely continue talking with smiles on their faces, and in time, they were sure to become fast friends. *She* would occupy the spot in Yulan that had been reserved for Violette until now.

She struggled to breathe. "Urk! Agh..."

As she vigorously stood up, the chair dragged across the floor, causing a cacophonous shriek to echo through the room. The dresser rattled but settled rather quickly thanks to its sturdy build.

Violette's heart, however, refused to settle down. She once again felt her chest tighten, along with an onslaught of nausea. Even though she didn't feel as though she would vomit up her food, she reflexively covered her mouth to prevent some ineffable thing from spilling out of her.

Slowly, very slowly, she steadied her breathing. She took deep breaths in through the fingers covering her mouth and exhaled little by little, striving to calm her tarnished thoughts and stabilize her consciousness.

How many seconds had it been? How many minutes? Maybe less time had passed than she had imagined. Violette didn't even have the energy left to keep track of time. That was how much of a shock, if not an outrageous disaster, this was.

Do I...want him all to myself?

Indeed, her fear stemmed from a very specific anxiety: she was terrified of Yulan being with Maryjune. Merely imagining it made her want to cry out. It was *she* who belonged at his side. Violette was feeling the powerful desire to hoard him for her own.

She clamped a voiceless scream between her teeth, causing it to reverberate through her body. Her fear was soon eroded, leaving behind a deep disappointment in herself.

Violette did not want to harbor these feelings. She'd sworn not to make the same mistake this time. Such a desire had been the catalyst that stained the end of her life. Her need to monopolize others' love and happiness had corrupted her former world. She should have known by now that her desire wouldn't make anyone happy—not even herself.

That was exactly why she had decided to devote her life to God.

Of all the people it could've been... Tch!

The hand covering her mouth snaked up to her forehead. She messed up her hair with abandon, unable to resist giving her tongue a vicious *click*. Her precious childhood friend had adored her since the day they met. She treated him like an adorable younger brother. She felt blessed just to watch over him as he slowly grew and matured.

She never once considered the thought of him being taken away.

"I'm sorry, Yulan."

Even Violette herself didn't understand why she would apologize when no one, not even the recipient, would ever hear it.

I Swear I Won't Bother You AGAIN!

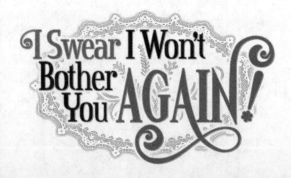

72 The Key to Reasoning

VIOLETTE KNEW OF TWO OUTCOMES that came from monopolizing someone. The first she had experienced herself, of course: the ending of a convict. The other was what came of a foolish woman who loved and pursued a single suitor... dwindling into a mere shadow of herself.

Until her dying breath, Violette's mother had yearned for one man, and she couldn't capture his heart even in death. She expected him to come back once she was bedridden and her life was in danger. Yet he didn't repay a lick of her feelings, and she had died alone.

This is just the worst.

Violette buried her face in her pillow, abandoning all hope of waking up. She was exhausted. Her body felt even heavier than before she fell asleep, meaning she probably had a nightmare. She couldn't remember any of it, unfortunately—or, perhaps, fortunately—but it must have been a fairly bad one.

She knew that she'd gotten so accustomed to the headaches and stomachaches that now she was practically numb to them.

The trade-off seemed to be that she felt more frequent, unfamiliar symptoms of intense stress and fatigue, so it was hard to judge whether this was an improvement or not. If asked, Marin would probably tell her that both were poison to her body.

With all this added pressure weighing her down, she had trouble getting up. Violette headed to her dresser with unsteady steps. Her stagger wasn't because she had barely woken up; she hadn't been able to rest and recover because of her nightmare.

"Just as I thought. I look a little swollen," she said to herself.

Looking in the mirror, she saw that her already pale complexion looked yet more pallid than yesterday; she would look as bloodless as a corpse next to a typical human. By contrast, her eyes looked painfully red. It was to be expected, given the intense pressure that lingered beyond them, but she hoped to get that redness relieved if possible—her troubled skin could be covered up with makeup to some extent. Marin would worry when she saw, but better to let her handle it. Marin was the type who would worry even more if Violette made her own inexpert attempts to mask the damage, and she'd likely expected this outcome anyway.

No, the real problem lay with someone else. Someone who understood Violette better than she understood herself.

Yulan's going to find out.

He would surely pick up even the faintest change in Violette. Even if her face hadn't been puffy with lack of sleep, the thickness of her makeup was sure to give it away. Normally, if she felt guilty for worrying him, she could laugh, thank him, and apologize, after which Yulan would reluctantly accept. Such an exchange could always put her heart at ease...but this time was different.

This was a feeling she had never harbored once since they met. She might distance herself from everyone else, but Yulan was special. And yet right now, she was afraid of seeing him. Just imagining his smiling face resurrected yesterday's fear. She was filled with terror at the idea that her desire would hurt him.

"What should I do?"

By the time Marin came calling, she still hadn't come up with a solution.

Yulan and Violette weren't entirely attached at the hip. He accompanied her often, but she assumed he had other friends and acquaintances to spend time with. While Yulan had never confirmed this, it was a fair notion considering his communication skills. He'd been by her side every day during the exam period, but everything should return to normal now that it was over.

Until yesterday, Violette never could've conceived that she'd feel relieved to have avoided him, or ever harbor such awkward emotions toward him.

The sigh that escaped her lips was louder than she had expected, but Violette was the only one around. This gazebo in the shade of the trees was always cleaned and maintained, but hardly anyone used it. It was tucked away, so few people knew it existed. The shade made it a little chilly too. Above all, while the gazebo was pretty, the surrounding nature had been left to its own devices. This corner was made to look picturesque, but it didn't have the ambience that would lure onlookers in.

Violette didn't want to believe that she was avoiding Yulan, but she couldn't very well deny it; after all, she had chosen a deserted spot she normally would've never visited. At the very least, she wanted to sort out her emotions. Guilt and self-hatred came over her from time to time, but now they were more potent than ever.

I don't even think there is a solution.

It wasn't as if something concrete had happened. She had merely noticed the feelings budding within her and then reacted to those feelings with dejection. Before she set about trying to deal with the issue, she would have to address that it existed. The one thing she was certain of was that she didn't want to shun Yulan...or, so she thought.

"I guess I was too naive."

Her self-deprecating laugh drifted through the lonely space. Apparently, her heart had suffered a graver wound than she realized. She leaned back against the bench and looked up, but a pure-white ceiling blocked her view of the sky. The gusts of wind that shook the trees were rather chilly, and passing clouds made the area grow a little darker.

It felt just like prison.

When she shut her eyes, she could vividly recall that day even now. Some pieces were missing, but the oath she'd made that day, her regret—all of that was carved into her heart, never to fade. But it still wasn't enough; she lacked determination. A mere feeling wouldn't be able to erase this well of desire on its own. That was exactly why she needed to fortify the logic that governed her feelings.

When Violette took a deep breath and opened her eyes once more, her delusion of living in a different world ended.

What lay within her heart could change drastically, and it could all be washed away just as easily. If she desired to stay true to something in spite of that, she must dedicate herself to it with all her might. She had one desire, one overriding emotion. She would not cause any harm to that girl.

I'll work as hard as I can...so I don't hurt her.

She would prove that she could control herself. She would work to erase her desire. Then, one day, it would be gone altogether. With her fists tightly clenched, she swore this, pretending not to notice the pain deep inside.

I Swear I Won't Bother You AGAIN!

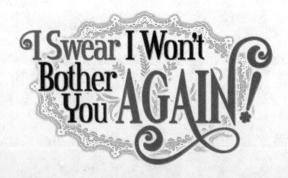

73 These First Few Seconds Will Be Known as "Fate"

VIOLETTE HEARD THE FAMILIAR crunching sound of footsteps.

"Huh?" came a surprised voice.

Violette whipped around immediately at the sound. It was shortsighted to assume that no one else would come here. She was here herself, after all; it made sense for someone else to sneak away in hope of avoiding other people. She was far more surprised when she saw the intruder's face, as it was one she recognized.

"Princess Rosette," Violette said.

"Oh...Lady Violette."

Rosette had as sweet and lovely an aura as usual. Gorgeous purple hair fluttered beautifully down her back. Her hair was the envy of all who beheld it—impossibly straight, with nary a wave nor curl in sight. Her smile and wide-open lavender eyes gave off a different impression than usual, most likely because the former failed to reach the latter. Her smile sat atop the panicked face of someone unsure what to do next.

"Um…"

Rosette clutched the object in her arms closer to her chest, her eyes darting to and fro. Violette didn't know this girl enough to understand if there was a deeper meaning to it, but it was clear that Rosette felt troubled by Violette's presence.

"My apologies. I'll be leaving soon," Violette told her.

"Oh!"

Violette was well accustomed to people disliking her by now. She no longer felt hurt by it, so nowadays she didn't even bother to contest their dislike. Such opinions hardly even registered to her now, as long as she didn't have to suffer others' malice directly.

She stood up and tried to walk by the princess.

"N-no, wait!" Rosette called out.

Right as she caught Violette by the arm, the book she'd been carrying fell to the ground.

Violette was confused. "Um…?"

"Ah, I'm sorry. Don't worry about that."

They both hurried to pick it up, when their hands bumped against each other and froze in place. One—Rosette—was jerky and unnatural in reaching toward the book, while the other—Violette—retained her typical grace. Both looked down at the open pages being caressed by the wind. Violette had taken it for a novel or something like that, but she could see a rainbow of colors inside. It wasn't a picture book, surprisingly.

"A field guide?" Violette murmured.

Rosette gasped. She visibly flinched at the sight of Violette processing the book's contents, and her outstretched fingertips

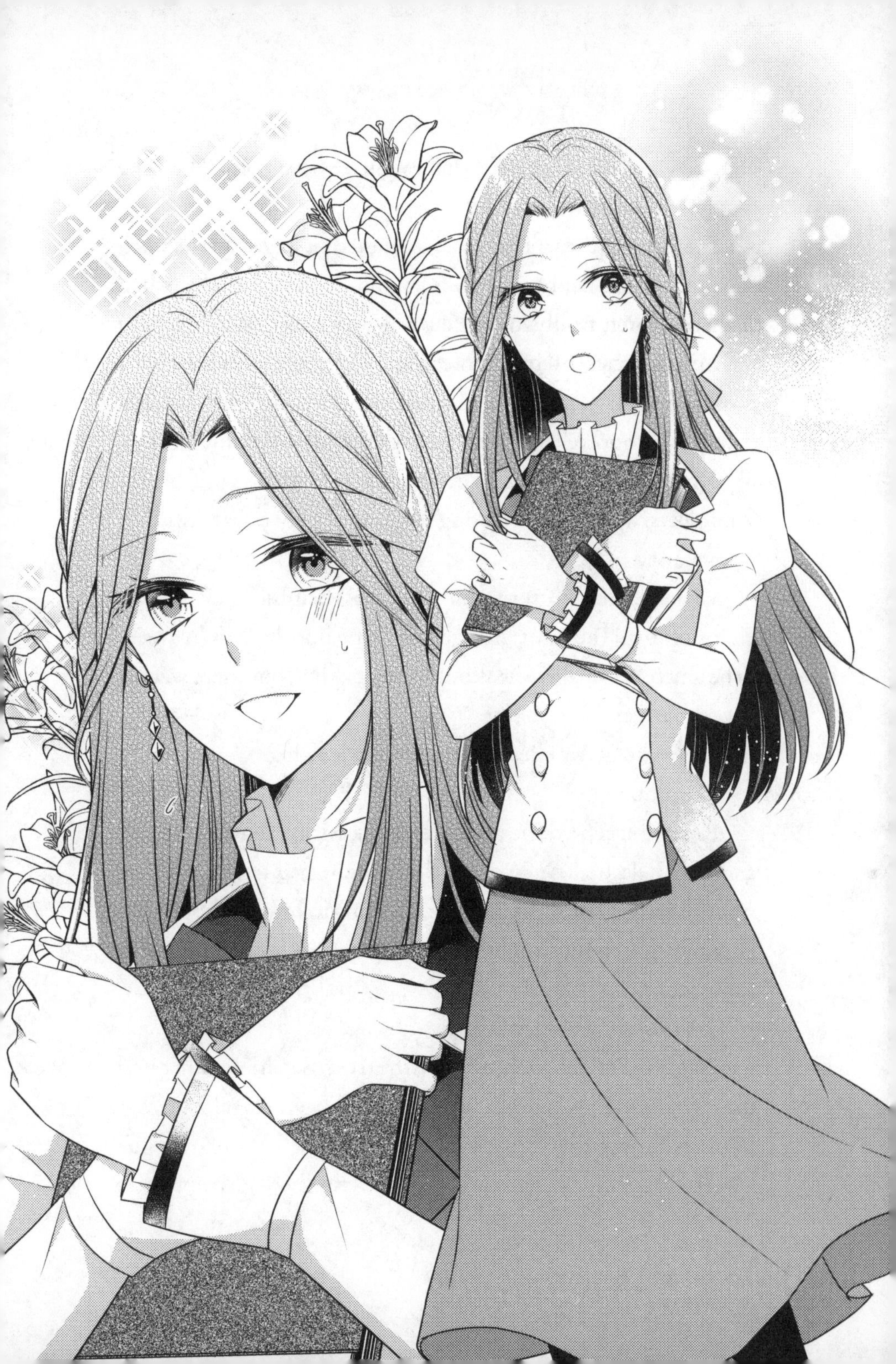

had been trembling for some time. Violette wasn't sure if holding that pose was painful for her.

There were many pictures and detailed passages on the open pages. It was similar to the books her mother had given her when she was young, back when she was being raised as a boy. That was exactly why Rosette's possession of the book was very unexpected. It wasn't simply a field guide but one with a very peculiar focus. The impression Rosette gave to the masses was surely that of someone who turned pages vibrantly painted with beautiful flowers. Violette had thought the same when watching her from afar.

Violette picked up the book for her, brushing off the fine grains of dirt. The cover had gotten dirty, but there didn't seem to be any real damage. She skimmed through it, but there weren't any torn pages.

"Here you go," Violette said, handing it to her.

"Oh, um, right."

Rosette accepted the presented book with an awkward lurch and then held it close. Violette thought she had tensed up from surprise earlier, but she must've been trying to hide the book. Her efforts had been for naught if so, now that the contents had been exposed.

"Er, this is..." Rosette began.

Try as she might to come up with an excuse, she couldn't find the right words. Now that her secret had been revealed, it was pointless to try to deceive Violette. Thus, she held her tongue. Violette perfectly understood her because she had been there before. She knew what the princess was feeling and what she wanted to say.

"You don't have to explain," Violette said. "I won't pry or say a word to anyone."

"What?"

"If you tell me to forget about it, I will. You don't want people to know, right?"

When they'd first laid eyes on each other, Rosette hadn't only felt uncomfortable because someone was here. Anyone's presence would have flustered her, but her panic intensified when she saw it was Violette, the subject of a number of unsavory rumors.

"You tried to stop me because you thought I'd get the wrong idea."

Rosette had realized that Violette would misunderstand and think that the princess hated her, so she grabbed her arm to dispel that idea. Unfortunately, it came at the cost of exposing her secret. No one was in the wrong here; it was merely the forces of coincidence at work. Rosette's anxiety didn't seem to subside, even so.

"Thanks for that," Violette continued. "I apologize for disturbing you."

She took no pleasure in exposing people's secrets. Truth be told, she wasn't interested in them at all. Violette's words didn't sound terribly persuasive, especially given that they were relative strangers, but she could only hope Rosette would believe her.

"You don't feel...disillusioned or anything?" Rosette asked.

"About what?"

"I mean, I..."

"I suppose it is a little unusual, maybe..."

The title of the book Rosette was holding read *Reptile Field Guide*. Such tomes were generally unpopular with the students. Many of them loved flowers and enjoyed nature, but insects and reptiles were generally considered separate. While the academy was rich in greenery and plants, it was rare to spot the wildlife that typically lived alongside them. They may occasionally intrude from outside, but they didn't tend to breed inside the academy grounds. It made sense that the academy students, regardless of their age or gender, would be disgusted by such creatures.

"...But you're free to enjoy whatever you like."

One person's likes were another's dislikes, and vice versa. There was no decree that required someone to only love the things everyone else did. People had the right to make their own choices, to decide their own preferences. Sure, people could hide those preferences, but there was no reason to force them to change.

"Some people really can't deal with them, though, so just be considerate of that."

Having the freedom to enjoy things was a completely different matter from being considerate of your surroundings. Forcing your passions on others only made you a pest. Past Violette hadn't understood that. She'd imposed her favorite things upon others, forced people to fit her needs, and it had all come back to hurt her in the end. It felt like all of this had occurred long ago, but she still recalled with perfect clarity the bloodlust she'd clutched on to that day.

Violette offered a quick bow and said, "Anyway, have a good day." Then she walked away without looking back.

This accidental encounter was soon pushed into the furthest reaches of her mind. It didn't have nearly enough impact to clear the swirling mist of her thoughts. However, Rosette's name grew more vivid in her mind, making this a possibly fortuitous meeting.

I Swear I Won't Bother You AGAIN!

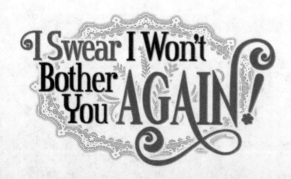

74 Perfect Idol

I N ROSETTE'S OPINION, perfection meant never straying from what people expected of you. "Pure," "beautiful," "adorable," "wonderful," and "ideal"—the plethora of compliments piled up and smothered her. They crushed her real self-image. By the time she realized how much it hurt, her body was already submerged past the point of escape. She didn't mind her name, so reminiscent of roses, but being likened to a flower was terribly constricting.

I guess it's not here this time either...

In middle school and even after entering high school, she would go check every time she heard that a new book had come in, only to be disappointed every time. This academy's libraries boasted an enormous collection in comparison, which included specialized books from all fields. That was why they had what Rosette desired.

However, they were still only technical books. They contained detailed passages regarding elaborate research, so it was questionable how much a hobbyist could find enjoyment in them. Rosette preferred illustrations to text, though she liked photographs best of all. Unfortunately for her, these tomes usually prioritized text over the other two.

"If you're looking for something, I shall help you, Lady Rosette!" one student offered.

"If there's something you'll be reading, we would like to try reading it too," said another.

"I'd also like to hear your recommendations," added a third.

"Thank you, everyone, but it's fine. I only came here to check out the new books," Rosette told them.

The students gazing upon her with shining eyes had already imagined the kind of recommendations Rosette would give. The Rosette in these girls' minds would surely suggest a sweet, heart-throbbing love story or a collection of scenic photographs. If she were asked for something unexpected, she would certainly choose an esoteric mystery novel of some sort.

Suddenly, someone let out a scream.

"Eek!"

"Hey, who was the one who left the window open?!"

Rosette turned to see people fleeing one corner of the room. A small creature was loitering close by the abandoned books and notebooks. Judging by its size, it was most likely a young lizard. Swinging its four legs as it walked, it didn't look like it would harm anyone. It was so small that it wouldn't do much of anything if left alone.

"What should we do?"

"I'll go call for someone."

This little guy would never be welcomed in the academy. Once discovered, his kind was always removed from the premises. The students screamed and ran, waiting for the adults to set the lizard free outside. Lizards didn't have the best reputation here; most people held unpleasant feelings toward them. They wouldn't be killed, but they certainly weren't welcomed to live on the grounds, either. One was expected to revile them, in short, and especially if one was a well-known lady.

"Are you okay, Lady Rosette?" a female student called out, her expression clouded with worry.

Rosette was frozen to the spot. "I am, thanks."

Surely, this girl also wasn't very good at dealing with reptiles either. She was likely the gentle sort who was always considering other people's feelings. It was a magnificent virtue to have. If her concern had been directed toward anyone else, it wouldn't have caused them pain.

Rosette was silent.

What face would this girl make if she knew? What if she discovered what the real Rosette—the girl's ideal princess—loved more than anything else? How would this girl see her? Would she still look at her with such kindness?

She imagined the response...and, without telling anyone, left the space.

Rosette believed it all started with her brothers' influence. Her two older brothers greatly indulged their youngest sister. They wanted to be with her at all times when they were young. Whether they were sleeping, eating, or playing, she would do everything while holding her brothers' hands. They played in the library rather than the garden, because her brothers knew the little princess couldn't be seen running around covered in mud. They may have been princes, but her brothers were still boys.

She loved the stories her brothers read to her, but reading tended to bore children, especially when they were young. Rosette wasn't the type to sit quietly with a book to begin with, so to hold her interest, the brothers overturned the whole library and read to her from every genre. They started with cute picture books, moved on to bittersweet love stories, stories on friendship, and fantasy, and even went as far as poetry anthologies.

Rosette couldn't remember when her brothers finally resorted to the field guides they personally owned, but she became entranced by their contents. They had large photographs accompanied by dense explanations. Occasionally, there were pictures of grotesque creatures, but she thought them lovely in their own way. Once she was able to read by herself, she grew interested in their ecology as well.

Every day, the three of them got together and immersed themselves in their field guides. By this time, it was more that the brothers were tagging along with their younger sister. Still, she never once called the creatures in these books "weird." She never condemned, disdained, or demoralized any of them.

She began to realize the sad truth: that being a princess who loved reptiles wouldn't be well received by others.

I Swear I Won't Bother You AGAIN!

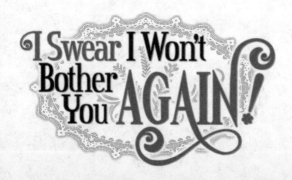

75 Idol Admiration

THE FIRST TIME ROSETTE realized something was wrong was when she was separated from her brothers and spoke with other girls.

She wore adorable clothes and accessories as instructed, but she had absolutely zero interest in them. As the other children her age complimented one another's dresses in delight, she could only give vague smiles, unable to keep pace. The many frills and ribbons were cute, in her opinion, but she didn't enjoy how they restricted her movements. In the rare case that an outfit did catch her eye, it still didn't dazzle her enough that she'd pick it out to wear. She could only ever see dressing up as her duty.

Girls loved cute things. They didn't like insects and reptiles. Girls thought flower gardens in bloom were beautiful. They weren't fascinated with vibrant, poisonous mushrooms. Girls wouldn't care about any gem that wasn't polished, no matter how pure its ore.

The more Rosette learned about girls and the ideal princesses these girls dreamed about, the further away she felt from that ideal. Fortunately, her appearance alone was close enough to the image everyone had of a perfect princess. She only had to fit into that mold to uphold their expectations.

Over time, her true self began to deviate from everyone's ideal. Even though she was the same "Rosette," she felt like there were two different people with that name. She had resigned herself to this almost as soon as she noticed it, so it didn't feel fair to get upset over it. However, one thing remained unresolved. Was there any need to keep the other Rosette around, flawed as she was?

Even though she was self-conscious about her true self, she couldn't hold it back. She couldn't change it. Nor did she have the intention to. As much as it hurt her to hide under her facade, and despite the fear of being found out, she refused to abandon herself. She must have known, somewhere in her heart—that one day, a day like this would come.

⚜

The package that came that day was the book Rosette had asked for, given to her under the pretense of a present from her brothers. It was hard to get her hands on at the academy...and even if it *were* there, she could never pick up such a book herself. It was an encyclopedia that didn't only concern reptiles but insects and poisonous plants too. In short, it was too far removed from the image of a perfect princess. She couldn't even claim to be using it to study; the subject matter was far outside the realm of possible coursework.

Still, she couldn't help where her passions lay. Her eyes naturally sought them out, her hands would reach out for them unbidden. It was pointless to resist. Fortunately, her brothers knew of her hobby and accepted her as their darling Rosette. That alone reassured her.

If she so chose, she could ignore everything and enjoy life without a care. She could cast aside the guilt that dogged her. Inside her mind, she could stand tall as the Rosette she really was. In her own world, she could follow her heart.

Sadly, she was always reminded that it was only pretend.

"Huh?"

She had assumed, somewhat foolishly, that no one would be here because she never saw anyone there until now. This dim place, where the earthy smell of dirt and leaves overpowered the fragrance of flowers, was a favorite of hers. No one came anywhere near here, and it was a fine place to observe the tiny intruders from time to time. This spot killed two birds with one stone.

But this time, a lady was sitting there.

Like a jewel inlaid with clouds, she gave off a striking impression even in the dark. The aura emanating from her made Rosette feel that this space belonged to her. No location would ever be considered an ill-fitting backdrop to this girl. She didn't exactly blend in; rather, she made the surroundings adapt to her.

Even her surprised expression was beautiful.

"Oh...Lady Violette."

Everyone knew that name. Violette ensnared the gazes of onlookers, luring them in and repelling them all at once. They would freeze, eyes locked on hers, wishing to be reflected in them. Rosette had only talked to her a handful of times, but she knew of all the rumors that plagued the girl. Though little more than surface-level gossip, many considered them true. Rosette was inclined to believe them, herself.

Fear struck her. Realizing Violette would read it in her face, she panicked, and that moment of weakness caused her to slip up. Violette's presence here had certainly frightened her, but it wasn't because it was *her* specifically. For a brief moment, Rosette's priorities were in flux.

"A field guide?" Violette asked.

Rosette didn't realize how deluded she had been until it was too late. She understood all at once how much regret a single slip could cause. Imagining how Violette's face might contort, her image of Rosette in tatters, sent ice running through her veins—she was terrified of being denied. Her mind raced with visions of her future, shredded to pieces by those beautiful lips as they revealed Rosette's secret. What a painful reminder that her self-image was only an illusion.

"You're free to enjoy whatever you like," Violette said.

Violette wasn't trying to console Rosette. She was indifferent altogether, implying that Rosette wasn't worth holding to any certain standard. Rosette had come and gone from Violette's mind in an instant.

How Rosette's heart fluttered, to think that she wasn't a part of this lady's world. So desperate was she for Violette's departing figure to turn around that she couldn't look away.

A gravitational pull drew her in, a magnetism that Rosette simply could not resist.

She was reluctant to reach out to Violette, even so. All she wanted now was to become acquainted with her. Rosette projected her dreams, her delusions, and everything else she had upon Violette's retreating back. The panic that always lurked in her breast had been replaced by something else. Only then did she realize what it was.

Ah... I admire her.

I Swear I Won't Bother You AGAIN!

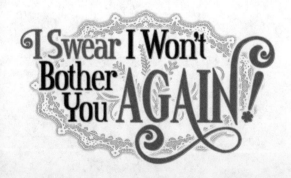

76 Hurting Rather Than Helping

VIOLETTE HAD NEVER BEEN GOOD at avoiding people. This normally would be considered a praiseworthy trait, but ultimately it gave people more reason to keep away from her, so she had mixed feelings about it. Her limited chances to interact with others had, ironically enough, helped her learn the art of closing off her heart. She didn't care to reflect on that too much. She learned the knack of making her way through with minimal interaction despite this, either by clearing her mind and letting their words pass over her, or by finding some way to excuse herself. Her methods varied based on the time, place, and target of a given chat.

Not that it mattered. The topics that people discussed, what they wished to tell her, and their impressions of her—all of it was trivial. People might take it on themselves to discuss Violette, to insist they were speaking in her best interest, but their words were hollow. She could give her own shallow responses in turn. She didn't engage them in conversation, nor think it necessary.

She had no idea how to act when directly facing another, trying not to hurt them with your words. She didn't even know what it meant to have a sincere heart-to-heart with someone. She had never considered such things before now.

"Found youuu!"

"Oh, Yulan…"

She could not think of any way to protect this gentle smile.

✦

Violette had assumed she could make it to the end of the day without running into Yulan. She hoped to see him tomorrow, after calming down a bit more. She cursed her optimism.

"What's wrong?" Yulan asked.

"Huh? Oh, um, it's nothing."

Her face had flickered with bewilderment for the briefest of moments. No one but Yulan would have noticed, usually, which may be why it had slipped out. This was exactly why she didn't want to see him right now. She felt like she might be sick.

"How about you, Yulan? Do you need something?"

"I wouldn't say *I* need anything…" Yulan said.

Violette bit back the urge to chew at her lips. Her expression was no longer her only concern; she had to watch her choice of words too. She knew her expression looked forced, but she couldn't get rid of her emotions right now. Not while she was still in a state of abject terror, struggling to come to terms with her situation and find a solution. If only she could purge herself of these emotions and wipe her mind clean! They nestled stubbornly in the folds of her brain instead, entrenching themselves deeper and deeper. She never imagined a day would come that she'd fear seeing herself in Yulan's gaze.

"Thought so," Yulan said. He reached out toward her face.

Violette didn't react to his approaching fingers until it was too late. "Ngh!"

The soft sensation of them brushing the bags under her eyes revealed how worried he was. She wasn't sure whether the cool sensation meant Yulan was cold or that her own eyes were too hot.

"You didn't get much sleep last night, did you?"

His concerned expression brought the pain rushing back, but all she could think about was how sweet and affectionate his touch was. She craned her neck to see his face. He had graduated from an adorable boy to a mature young man. He was no longer the one being doted upon; now he was kind and considerate of others. That was surely something beautiful and proved that a cute boy could grow into a wonderful man. She should have been delighted about it.

"Vio...?"

Violette's breath hitched.

"What happened?"

His question came out as more of a demand. The heavy tone suggested that he knew something had happened to her. She wasn't surprised that he'd noticed. Quite the opposite, even. She expected him to pick up on it without a shadow of a doubt.

"It's... It's nothing. I'm fine."

If she took a step back, she would be leaving his warmth. Her forced smile warped further; she could tell she looked anything but fine. Nothing *was* fine, and she couldn't even explain why.

"The chauffeur is already waiting, so I need to go now," she told him.

"What? But—"

"See you later, Yulan."

The way she forcibly concluded the conversation was utterly unnatural, but she didn't have time to consider it now. She pressed on with her departure, despite his obvious desire to say something. She knew how shifty she was being, but she had to disappear from his sight. She didn't *want* to avoid him. Honestly, she wanted to turn around and walk back to him. But she didn't know what else to do.

She was delighted to see how much Yulan had grown. All this time, she had dreamed of watching him find happiness from afar. That is, the moment he found someone he treasured. And yet, Violette didn't want to imagine his smile, his voice, his touch, or his heart to go to anyone but her. She wished she'd never realized how she truly felt. Now that she had awakened to this selfish desire, Yulan was the last person she wanted to see it.

77   Leviathan's Breath

LEFT BEHIND, YULAN RUMINATED on Violette's appearance in silence. He was adrift in a noxious mixture of shock and despair. He furrowed his brow; he was standing, but he might collapse at any moment. He doubted anyone would see the raised corners of his mouth as a smile. It certainly didn't stand a chance of convincing himself of its sincerity.

He could easily have chased after her, but what was the point? Without a plan, he'd only be playing games with her heart. He didn't need to chase after and press her with questions but contemplate the root cause of this sudden panic that haunted Violette's features.

Family matters, maybe? No, it's a little different.

It wouldn't be the first time that house had been a bed of thorns to Violette. It never gave her the briefest moment of peace. Infuriating as that was, it also meant that nothing in her home life could have rattled her this much. No matter how shocking the events under that roof were, she had resigned herself to being a spectator. She would snuff out her feelings without fail and wait for the storm to pass, protecting herself from the deluge of pain.

Then what is it? Does it have to do with me? No, probably not.

Few factors could so thoroughly disturb the normally calm and quiet Violette. Could it be Claudia?

No, that probability was low. Violette in her current state made her former self, the one that rampaged around in a love-drunk haze, seem like an illusion. Yulan wasn't sure if her meekness stemmed from a change in her approach or if her love had simply cooled down. The latter was closer to the truth, but he had no way to know that. It was hard, even so, for Yulan to blame Claudia for disturbing her heart this time.

Did I do something? No, that can't be it.

The last time they met, Violette was smiling cheerfully. He would've noticed right away if she had been faking it. He made it a habit to be fully tuned in to her subtleties and went out of his way to eliminate her sorrows. Naturally, Yulan knew the limits of what he could do, but he still took pride in his ability to provide her even the slightest escape.

The fact remained that he, himself, was the most likely reason for Violette to be so unsettled in his presence.

That guy's the only other thing between us, though.

The beautiful prince's silhouette flashed in Yulan's mind. He'd discarded Claudia as a candidate, but he *was* deeply connected to both Yulan and Violette. He shouldn't have had anything to do with this, though. Violette had already rejected him.

In that case, could it be Claudia's best friend, Milania? No, not him either. Milania's words and demeanor were never enough to upset Violette, even if it was related to Yulan—no, even more so if Yulan was involved. Yulan could easily imagine Violette dealing with Milania with no issue.

All that left was his own friend, Gia...but that was absolutely impossible. While Gia lived life on his own terms and did things even Yulan couldn't understand, he had little interest in other people. Gia was much more of an observer. He had no interest in the rumors surrounding Yulan and Violette; he wouldn't intentionally light a fire under her. Besides, Violette hadn't opened up to Gia yet. Someone so distant wouldn't have such a deep effect on her.

Who else? If someone out there can upset her this much, I should definitely know who they are.

Reaching a dead end, he sighed. He leaned against the window frame and absentmindedly looked up at the ceiling. He stifled the sound of his tongue clicking, irritated at this unknown enemy. Possible suspects continued to appear and disappear one after another, narrowing down little by little. He had unconsciously excluded a number of targets who held no interest to him.

This person had to be someone who made Violette miserable and a person who knew of Yulan. Personally, he viewed the mob around him as worthless trash. He hated the Vahan family, but he didn't pay them any particular mind as individuals. They were merely a collection of unbelievably stupid, ignorant, and obnoxious people.

Right then, he heard Maryjune's voice. "Yulan! Are you going home now?"

"Yeah, I'm about to."

Most people might liken Maryjune's smile to flowers dancing in the air. Her brilliant blue eyes sparkled, and every strand of her hair swaying in the breeze was beautiful. What kind of aspirations did people have for this girl that she would be so showered in love, steeped in it, and raised so tenderly?

"Um, if you don't mind, can we talk for a bit?" Maryjune asked.

"Fine. Just for a little while."

Maryjune's smile gained another level of radiance at Yulan's response. Surely, many would envision a large sunflower blooming behind her—a backdrop to befit this bright, gentle, and lovely girl. Yulan, by contrast, imagined a thick, black serpentine beast capable of snapping Maryjune's neck in an instant. He pictured his words taking shape and wrapping around her fragile throat.

To Violette, Maryjune was a bomb that could explode anywhere, at any time. She was a devil of a girl; a harbinger of fear and foolishness that stuck her nose in every possible outcome, crushing every choice at her disposal. It must be her. The girl before him was the most likely culprit behind Violette's abnormal behavior.

That meant Maryjune was dragging Yulan into this. Maryjune was using Yulan to some end, though he wasn't sure if her plans centered around Violette or himself. He didn't know what Maryjune's intentions were, nor did he care. What *was* important was that Maryjune was using him to cause Violette harm in some way.

I'd better look into this more closely.

Yulan had to figure out what this girl was plotting. His whole being was devoted to eradicating Violette's sorrows, to paving her path to health and happiness. He had to figure out if Maryjune was one of those sorrows; if so, he'd need to deal with her as an individual rather than a member of the Vahan family.

Yulan needed to be ready to choke her dead with a single word.

I Swear I Won't Bother You AGAIN!

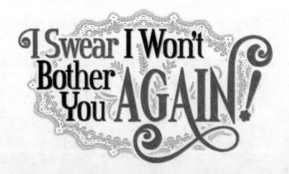

78 Beyond Good or Evil

VIOLETTE HAD NEVER RETURNED HOME this early of her own volition before. Not because she wanted to be here, of course—she couldn't bring herself to walk around the city without Yulan. It wouldn't be any fun without him. She wished she'd talked more with him then, or invited him out, but it was too late for regrets; she was already at the house. Most importantly, she was scared of what she might tell him after all that had happened.

Marin saw her complexion and immediately sensed that something was amiss. "Lady Violette..."

"I'm going to rest awhile," Violette told her.

"All right. I'll get things ready for you."

From the way she undressed herself to the way she changed into new clothes, Violette's every action was sluggish and slow, so Marin helped her. When Violette retired to the sofa, head nodding with drowsiness, Marin warmed some milk for her.

Though she knew her maid was taking great pains for her sake, Violette couldn't summon enough energy to respond. She couldn't thank Marin for making the drink, or even relish its sweet flavor. Unable to find repose or reset her thoughts, she couldn't reassure Marin she was all right or even give her a smile.

Sleep was impossible. All she could manage was to close her eyes.

⚜

Warm milk with plenty of honey was one of Violette's favorites. The head chef taught Marin how to make it after she'd badgered him numerous times, and countless hours of practice later, she ended up with a signature take on the drink that Violette adored.

This girl was so battered and broken down that the only way she knew how to comfort herself was to cower in place. Marin wanted to make her smile more than anything, but she had no idea how. She announced one day that she would put together a platter of Violette's favorite treats, no matter how extravagant. It was heartbreaking to see Violette smile solely out of consideration for her feelings.

The treat that finally did the trick was warm milk loaded with spoonfuls of honey. It was awfully sweet compared to regular warm milk, and Violette enjoyed it all the more if given time to cool. As adorably kitten-like as Violette looked when lapping at hot beverages, her tender smile when drinking one without any steam filled Marin with euphoria. When she first saw the tension in Violette's shoulders relax as she sipped the drink, she was relieved to the point of tears. The only one who knew this was the head chef, whom Marin had clung to when she actually cried.

Marin made her special warm milk over and over again after that. When she first realized that all the cups of warm milk in the world wouldn't wash away every agony that Violette faced, Marin was tempted to blame her own lack of skill. Her first attempts were total failures and her techniques had been atrocious, but now she could whip up perfect cups of warm milk with her eyes closed—through it all, what mattered was that her mistress enjoyed it. Violette's smile let Marin take pride even in her greatest failures. Violette's smile was like a gentle "thank you," assuring her she'd done a good job.

She...didn't touch it.

Marin left the room, carrying Violette's school uniform, and recalled her mistress holding her breath behind her.

Why?

This had never happened before. Violette should have reached out for the cup, wrapped both hands around it to feel its warmth, and relaxed. She didn't need to drink it right away, but she should still have smiled and thanked Marin.

"Tch."

The dull sound of Marin's clenched teeth grinding against one another stifled the sound of her clicking tongue. She was aware that her brows were furrowed; her expression must have looked frighteningly grim.

A scene from yesterday appeared in her mind unbidden: that pearl-colored girl with her innocent smile.

That bitch!

No servant of an aristocratic household would dare use such foul language, but Marin thought she deserved praise for not saying it aloud. Had she not such a firm grip on her work mentality, she would've headed straight to Maryjune and beaten her until she was satisfied.

Marin had no idea of the swirling chaos in Violette's mind. She could never have imagined that Violette was battling the desire within herself to hoard Yulan for her own. Still, she easily identified the cause of Violette's strange behavior.

Ever since Violette left the dinner table yesterday, she'd been acting strange. Specifically, she went pale as soon as Yulan's name left Maryjune's lips, and her color had yet to return. She assumedly suffered nightmares because of it, judging by how her face in the morning looked worse than before she went to bed. Her half sister's statement was the obvious cause. It infuriated Marin more than anything.

Maryjune probably didn't put much thought into her words. Such a pure, naive creature could never conceive of hurting someone with her actions, not if she had their best interests at heart. If she did make a mistake and hurt someone, she'd surely assume that a simple "I'm sorry" would make everything right again. Every atom of Maryjune proclaimed that people were inherently good. She was a virtuous girl to the core.

So, what the hell was wrong with her?

Virtuous people weren't immune to using their innate goodness as a cudgel. Someone could take a million lives and still be seen as a hero; others could be branded a murderer after claiming just one. Maryjune was a good person. There was no malice in her statement. Violette had been wounded of her own accord.

What does that matter?

Marin hated Maryjune more than any criminal. She resented her, scorned her. Maryjune could be the heroine who had defeated the demon lord or the patron saint of the country—no matter how beloved or respected for her actions she might be, Marin's hate wouldn't waver. Nor did she care if that hatred marked her as a sinner.

No matter what anyone said, in Marin's eyes, Maryjune was evil.

I Swear I Won't Bother You AGAIN!

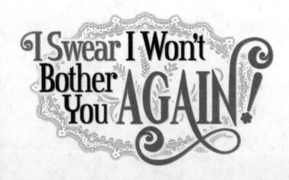

79 Perception and Perspective

As MARIN SPEWED OUT SILENT CURSES, Maryjune was still in the academy. Maryjune was the opposite of Violette, often heading straight home instead of staying out late. The sisters had swapped habits just for today; despite a quarter of blood running in their veins being identical, the two girls couldn't be less alike.

Yulan looked at Maryjune's smiling profile. He knew he would never care about this girl, whether she resembled her half sister or not.

"You've been friends with my sister for a long time, right?" Maryjune asked him.

"Yeah... It's not just us, though. Most students in the academy have been acquainted with one another for a long time."

Yulan spoke with a smile as radiant as Maryjune's own...or so it would appear to any of his typical, everyday acquaintances. If Gia were here, however—or even Claudia—they would notice the lack of any emotion beyond the nigh-invisible mask on his face.

The beautiful parabola drawn by his lips. His narrowed eyes. His composed tone. His perfect countenance. Anyone who saw him would think he was smiling; any who disagreed would be deemed crazy. That was why his expression fit so poorly. The real Yulan lacked any gentleness whatsoever. Even Gia, whom everyone considered his best friend, hardly ever witnessed Yulan's smile. Underneath the several thousand layers of faces, there existed a heartless, merciless, aloof person who could bring a demon to tears.

This man would only ever show a heartfelt smile to one person: Violette. The moment he left her company, Yulan's face became a void. However soft and gentle of an expression it was or how flawless it appeared, not a fragment of emotion remained after closer scrutiny. His expressions were layered paint on top of the mask, depicting appropriate faces for any occasion.

"So they made friends back in middle school, did they? I wonder if people stop making friends once they get to high school," Maryjune mused aloud.

"There are some exceptions to the rule, no?"

"You think?"

Yulan wasn't particularly interested in Maryjune. An upstanding person would no doubt feel sympathetic to the obviously despondent girl and recognize her as a victim for being thrown into the aristocratic world with no knowledge of her parents' circumstances.

However, Yulan was not an upstanding person at all.

What a waste of time.

He didn't feel saddened by her dejected look; if anything, he was ready to click his tongue at her for messing with him and forcing his participation in this meaningless conversation.

He'd gleaned how naive and pure Maryjune was from their chat. She might be bright and loving, but that guaranteed she would be the type of person who lacked discretion.

Such people never so much as contemplated widening their outlook. They valued benevolence as good, considered the majority rule equality, and treated the reformation of heretics as righteous. Blind to the oppressed, they smiled in their ignorant belief that the world was a happy place. They surely wouldn't even notice if a corner was shaved away. They believed that by making everything in their view beautiful, they were also making the world beautiful. They wouldn't realize how dangerous their mindset was. No matter how far they extended their hands, they couldn't fully envelop everything in their arms.

If this was the philosophy Maryjune held, then it was pointless for Yulan to observe her any longer. If the girl herself didn't care to notice the world around her, then it wouldn't matter what suppositions or explanations Yulan provided for her benefit. Their fundamental worldviews would never agree.

He said, "I'm sorry, but are you done? I left a bunch of stuff in the classroom so I want to go back."

"Oh, I see! I'm sorry. Thank you."

"No problem."

Unlikely as Maryjune was to provide more information, accompanying her any further would be a waste of time. Not only did he lack any positive feelings toward her, but they were incompatible. Their personalities were hopelessly mismatched. He raised himself up from leaning on the window frame.

As Yulan turned around without saying farewell, her lovely voice called out after him.

"I'm glad I got the chance to talk to you! Can we do this again?"

"We're in different classes. Also, wouldn't it be better to talk with other girls?"

"Not at all! We finally got the opportunity to get to know each other. I hope we can talk a lot and become friends."

"I see."

"Yeah! It was a pleasure, Yulan!"

She waved, said that she would see him again tomorrow, and disappeared. All the while, Yulan remained planted to the spot.

A shocking outcome, indeed. He was astonished, to tell the truth. It had all happened so suddenly; he hadn't even considered that this might happen.

"Pfft... Ha ha ha!"

He brought a hand to his lips, but a laugh spilled out from the gaps between his fingers. This was a rare laugh, straight from his heart. There was no mask—it was a display of Yulan's true feelings.

That girl is too funny!

"Aah, hilarious."

After laughing for some time, Yulan's face twisted in ambivalence. The depths of his eyes were ice cold, but distinct evidence of a smile remained on his mouth. He knew that the girl was an imbecile. In Yulan's opinion, pure and honest people were the greatest fools of all. He'd grown to look down on them, wishing to trample them underfoot.

It appeared that this girl was far, far more thickheaded than Yulan had imagined.

Friends, huh?

As if such a day would ever come. Yulan would never see any greater worth in Maryjune; he couldn't envision any way for her to prove useful. That benevolent girl would never understand the feelings of a man who would annihilate anything for Violette's sake—especially since he had already determined that he would destroy Maryjune too.

He wondered if the girl in question would ever realize that.

No, she wouldn't. Until the day Yulan bared his fangs, the girl would believe in him unerringly. She would trust that everyone experienced the same gentle world as her. Unaware of the underside of reality, unable to appreciate how narrow her own outlook was, Maryjune could only conceive of pure, righteous, and beautiful things. Her smile was ignorant of the line between dreams and reality.

Everything would be over before Maryjune realized that, from when she first spoke to him to when she said farewell, Yulan hadn't once ever intended to see eye-to-eye with her.

I Swear I Won't Bother You AGAIN!

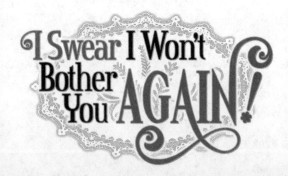

80 A Storm of Change

WHEN VIOLETTE REALIZED she couldn't sleep, it made it even harder for her to do so. The more flustered she got, the further into a corner she was driven. She didn't know if she had only closed her eyelids or if she'd actually slept; all she knew was that when morning came, she only felt more exhausted. If this continued, her body wouldn't be able to take it. She slept when she lost consciousness, but that hardly counted as rest.

Violette endured a heavy feeling, different from her normal weight or the pull of gravity; it was as though her guts were filled with stones. Her whole body felt crushed under some invisible pressure. She would have hung her head with a gloomy sigh had she been anywhere but her classroom in the academy; instead, she sat there in silence.

For better or worse, she was the very picture of melancholy. Violette's beauty made her downcast eyes staring into the void look charming, but she couldn't tell if the unnecessary attention she got from it was a help or a hindrance. It was even tougher to discern on a day like today.

Though she'd returned home early yesterday to avoid Yulan, she hadn't recovered at all. That much should have been a given, considering her house was as beneficial to her well-being as a poisonous bog. Still, she ought to have long since built up a resistance to it after the years of sleepless nights.

Thinking about her relationship with Yulan, and her newly realized emotions regarding it, would lead her brain to extrapolate every possibility at breakneck speed. Falling asleep would likely lead to terrifying nightmares. This left her unable to either sleep or faint.

Thanks to Marin's request to the head chef to provide smaller portions for her dinner and breakfast, Violette managed to finish her meals. And thank goodness; had Marin not been so perceptive, Violette would have been tortured by the ingredients as she forced them down her throat. She was grateful, but her heart also ached from the maid's consideration. She appreciated how much Marin cared for her. It was a shame that her maid couldn't fully dispel her grief.

Normally, it would be easier than this.

Violette would typically have given up on her desires more easily, or else come up with solutions sooner. She should have chosen the path among her limited choices that would hurt her the least, or followed orders obediently without thinking about it. Fretting wouldn't help matters; she needed to silence her heart and keep moving.

The same was required of her now. She mustn't think deeply about it. All she needed was to cast away these feelings, since they would only hurt Yulan. She would suffer no longer; she would feel no more pain. She was only required to spectate as her body's cells worked, processed, and gradually died. The best solution lay before her, clear as crystal...yet she somehow couldn't bring herself to put it into action.

I thought I didn't have any desire left in me.

The memory of her original sin bright in her mind, she assumed she'd already exhausted it all. Her repressed desires had instantly erupted out of her at that time and concluded her life in tragedy, but apparently the root of the issue hadn't changed.

Past Violette clung to her hope with all her might. She would take the faintest spark of light and her dreams would magnify it into a mighty sun. One day, she was sure of it, one day her prince would come to save her. She erroneously believed herself to be the heroine of a tragedy and that she would be paid in full for all the times she'd had to crush her own heart beneath her heel. She would get her happy ending. She would live happily ever after and let everyone bear witness. Happiness was a necessity for all heroines, so all her past trespasses would be forgiven. That was why she had continued to suffocate her own self all this time.

She could recognize now how ridiculous and foolish those thoughts were. Her simple yearning warped into something twisted. Her dreams overtook reality. A bad ending was an appropriate conclusion for a delusional heroine who believed she could make her ideals into a reality. Her reservoir of emotions empty, her heart crushed, she was already completely hollow inside. In exchange for the loss of her hopes and dreams, even her despair had been swallowed up. She no longer needed to aspire to anything nor be envious of anyone. She should have been able to relax and live without further complications after casting away such desires.

"...lette! Lady Violette!"

"Eep! Oh...I'm sorry. Yes?"

Nestled deep in her depressing thoughts, she had forgotten where she was. She already knew what kind of rumors would sprout if she acted so dejected in front of others.

The girl who'd called out to her was vaguely familiar to Violette, though she couldn't quite put a name to the face. This girl was no more than a classmate acquaintance, so not someone who would casually hold a conversation with her.

"Sorry for calling out to you so suddenly," the girl said. "Someone's here to see you."

"Me?"

Imagining who it could be slowed her movements. She wasn't sure how it had been for past Violette, but her current list of friends was shockingly tiny. It was limited to the people she interacted with, and she couldn't call any one of them a friend. Perhaps it was a family member? Although, then the girl would have said "your sister" rather than "someone," since many people were well aware of the Vahan family tree.

That left only one other candidate.

Had Yulan come to ask about what happened yesterday? She knew full well that she'd concluded their last conversation in an unnatural way, never mind the attitude she had when she tried to avoid him. Of course Yulan would be suspicious.

"Thank you for informing me," Violette said.

"Y-you're welcome!"

Violette threw a sidelong glance at the messenger, who appeared to be flustered about something. Her seat was awfully far from the door, yet she felt like she'd gotten there in a flash. If he *had* come, Violette didn't know what sort of emotions that might stir in her. Normally, she would have been delighted, but now? It was terrifying to her. Her chest was tight. Her delight was tempered by pain, her excitement curdled with dismay. Everything would be fine if she could just easily turn him away.

Tormented by these contradictions and conflict, she looked to the person outside the door.

"Wha...?"

She met the gaze of someone far shorter than she had expected, and she could only freeze in surprise and doubt. Her mind was crammed full of question marks that quieted her inner turmoil.

"Lady Rosette?"

"H-how do you do!"

Standing there with a stiff expression, trembling voice, and a rigid posture, was the princess.

I Swear I Won't Bother You AGAIN!

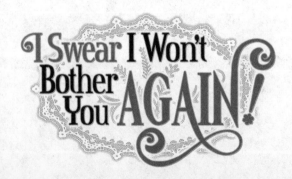

81 A Pair of Loners

VIOLETTE UNDERSTOOD WHY the surrounding eyes were filled with curiosity. Both she and Rosette attracted the attention of others, but when the overwhelmingly beautiful Violette and the bounteously dignified Rosette were together, it gave a completely different meaning to the concept. Both had attended the academy since middle school, though they rarely, if ever, spoke to each other. They had exchanged words and were aware of each other's existences, but their relationship never went past acquaintances. That hadn't changed—in Violette's mind, anyway.

I was so preoccupied with Yulan that I completely forgot about her.

Violette's focus hadn't been on her meeting with Rosette but rather on what had happened immediately after it. Up until this very moment, the encounter had been haphazardly stored in the corner of her memory. It hadn't been terribly significant.

It probably feels important to her, though.

Yesterday, Violette had accidentally learned Rosette's secret. To Violette, it was an inconsequential piece of information, easily forgotten; no misunderstandings would arise. But from Rosette's perspective, it must have been her worst fear.

Secrets were weaknesses. The fewer people who knew, the heavier it became to bear one; the mere act of keeping a secret felt like deceiving others. How terrifying it was to have others know that you kept such things hidden...and surely it felt even more so when your secret was uncovered by a demanding young lady who had nary a good word said about her in public. Rosette must have felt extremely uneasy.

Violette could sympathize. Even if she were in Rosette's position, she would have taken similar actions.

"Shall we go elsewhere for a bit?" Violette suggested.

"Ah, y-yes! Um, actually, I have a place in mind."

"Huh?"

It was Violette's turn to be perplexed. Rosette's shifty and uncertain behavior from moments ago had melted away—just what had brought on this change? Unable to summon any questions for the newly determined girl, Violette simply followed behind her.

⤜⧽⧼⤛

Their destination was a place she found quite familiar; they had met there just yesterday, in fact. This gazebo was undoubtedly a paradise where Rosette could safely disclose precious secrets. As usual, the area around them was slightly dim and felt deserted.

"Here?" Violette asked. "Why?"

Violette had assumed that Rosette would take her to an empty parlor, but it was true that this place was ideal to talk without prying ears. She never expected that she would revisit it, however, especially after what happened yesterday. Violette had intended to give it a wide berth from now on.

"This place is really unpopular. The shade makes it hard to see from outside...which is exactly why I come here often," Rosette explained.

"Oh?"

That meant that their encounter at that time wasn't as unfortunate of a coincidence. The two happened to bump into each other in a chance meeting, nothing more.

"That's why, um...I thought it might be the same for you."

Rosette stood still, a short distance before Violette, and slowly turned around to face her. Only the sound of the wind passing in between the two was crisp and clear; all other sounds were muted. Voices, gazes, anyone's ideals and impressions—none of them could reach here.

"I thought that...you might want to be alone. And that's why you'd come here."

That was Rosette's logic. She assumed Violette would see her as "stealing" this spot from her and that Violette would stop using the gazebo altogether if she knew Rosette visited it as well. Her prediction hit the target perfectly. She felt the same way—if Violette was going to come here for reprieve, it would be better for Rosette not to use it anymore.

These two people, so desperate to be alone, were able to understand each other's feelings.

"But then, where do you—"

"I-I know of many other places! Um, the places I enjoy aren't much favored by other people, so they'll certainly be unoccupied."

Rosette's giddy, bashful expression looked quite childish compared to her usual elegant countenance. This must be the real Rosette; she had lowered her guard now that her deepest secret had been exposed, for better or worse. Existing for the sake of others was painful. It had hardened her heart, made her feel as though she were being crushed or even torn apart.

"You don't need to worry about me," Violette told her.

"S-sorry?"

"You...are correct so far."

It *was* her desire to be alone that had led Violette to such a place. She'd wanted a spot free from anyone's gaze, expectations, impressions, or rumors...but that didn't necessarily mean she wanted a place where no one was around.

When she walked past Rosette, who was still staring straight ahead in her bewilderment, and into the gazebo, it was as though everything became darker. The sun was supposed to shine on everything equally, but the simple layering of trees had easily obstructed its light. The darkness, sure to be found gloomy by many, felt like protection to her. She wanted to avoid anyone who couldn't empathize, whether they meant her well or harm, for she found all emotions directed at her annoying. She craved to exist somewhere where her feelings couldn't be denied.

"Let's not stand around and talk. Please, sit."

"Huh?! Oh, um, all right!" Rosette peeped, flustered.

The abrupt change in her expression made Rosette adorable, in Violette's opinion. That observation alone proved she'd relaxed somewhat since yesterday, when her mind threatened to burst apart due to the many thoughts crammed within. Her thoughts may have stalled from Rosette's unexpected actions in a place she hadn't anticipated, but that was fine. Violette wanted to distance herself from reality and remain empty for a little longer. She would indulge this fellow loner for a short while.

I Swear I Won't Bother You AGAIN!

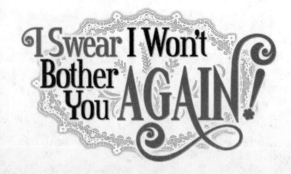

82   Tired of the Touching

SUDDEN CALM COULD COME at any moment: in the midst of a war, in the lull between violent attacks, even during a brief reprieve from pain. Violette was troubled to the point of insomnia, but she welcomed any sort of respite where she could catch her breath. This was one such opportunity.

"You are the princess of Lithos, right, Lady Rosette? It's no wonder you have such beautiful purple hair and eyes."

"Yes, although people with hair and eyes like mine are rare nowadays."

"Really? I've never been to your country...though I have seen a Lithosian jewel before."

A Lithosian jewel was a purple gem that could only be gathered in Lithos. It bore the country's name, and its brilliance was beautiful enough to attract anyone's eyes. Its average value was said to be three times that of a diamond.

Rosette's native country, Lithos, was a small nation but still popular among the rest. Many of its citizens had purple hair or eyes, hence why they bestowed their country's namesake upon this exclusive gemstone. Violette's knowledge on this subject was limited to textbooks and hearsay, but she'd heard such features were shared by almost everyone in Lithos. Hearing the truth was a reminder of how hard it was to discern rumors from facts nowadays.

"My brothers are twins, but one only has purple hair while the other has purple eyes. Their faces are mirror images of each other, though."

"Oh, then it must be easy to tell them apart," Violette remarked.

"Hee hee, that's what everyone says. They mustn't mistake the princes' identities, so it was a great relief for them."

"Yes, that is...rather important, indeed."

The smile that rose unbidden to Violette's lips was like a cruel joke at her own expense. She had no way of proving her own identity for herself. After budding, being born, and finally being given a name, her life had been acknowledged, addressed by that name, and ultimately molded into an individual. She would never become anything other than herself, no matter how much she adored, envied, and mimicked others; she would be a mere imitation. That was a wonderful thing in its way. A cruel, wonderful thing.

She couldn't become someone else, but she could still stand in for them. She could even transform elements about herself accordingly, when pushed, so she took it for granted and forgot that she couldn't manage more. Her inability to just *be* someone else had slipped her mind just like that.

"It is, but...that's exactly why I want something else to differentiate them," Rosette said.

Rosette thought it a smart choice to tell her brothers apart using the easiest method, as it meant she was far less likely to mix them up. At the same time, she wanted to go a step further and find some way to treasure them even more as individuals.

"I cherish those who are dear to me. I hate the idea of mixing them up without the colors of their eyes and hair to guide me."

It shouldn't be especially difficult. All she needed was to look at them more closely. Rosette's older brothers were two different people who'd been close with her ever since she was born.

"You seem close to your brothers," Violette observed.

"I am. We played together often when we were little. Being both the youngest and a girl, they were quite overprotective of me."

Watching Rosette's smile as she recounted her memories put Violette at ease, perhaps due to some self-indulgent sympathizing on her own part. If Violette had to liken the feeling to anything, it would be the tenderness she felt when reading a picture book.

"Did you get into your hobby because of your brothers?"

Rosette's expression froze for a moment. Her eyes flickered here and there, and even though she didn't have it on her now, she stared at the spot where she had been holding the guide yesterday.

"They might have...influenced me. The first book like that I ever saw was one of theirs."

"A lot of boys have them. I also had some when I was young," Violette told her.

"You too?"

"More precisely, they were my father's."

They were the same books her father had read when he was young which her mother had prepared for her. The actual copies her father had used were terribly deteriorated and unfit for reading, but Bellerose had easily ordered new ones from the publisher.

"I enjoyed the ore guide, so I read through it often. It was less the actual jewels that interested me and more the production sites and language of stones."

"Oh! M-me too!"

Little by little, the back-and-forth rally of their conversation continued. They slowly updated each other's boundaries and confirmed each other's limits. To avoid overstepping the line or stepping on toes, they conversed while carefully choosing their words; such restraint wore heavy on their hearts and minds and left them drained. Still, it was far, far more meaningful to spend their time this way when compared to their usual tactics of freezing their thoughts, suppressing their own hearts, and keeping their mouths firmly shut. This fatigue was comfortable, and neither had felt it in a very long time.

83 | A Tiny Dash of Spice

WHEN THE TWO OF THEM exhausted one topic, they smoothly moved on to another. It took quite some time to pass before Violette realized that this repeated cycle was known as "chatting." She had assumed this girl to be her polar opposite, but Rosette had quietly held her tongue while enduring hardship as Violette had. The more they talked, the more similarities Violette felt between their inner selves. Who would have imagined such a development between two girls who had assumed they shared nothing in common? Once Violette thought about it, however, it made quite a lot of sense.

Violette had been raised as a boy during her most influential stage of childhood, while Rosette possessed hobbies and preferences that were greatly removed from her image as the perfect princess. The two held on to things that detached them from the framework of a lady. Though their interests didn't exactly overlap, their kinship in this regard helped their talking points to converge smoothly.

"What causes me the most stress is having a new dress made," Rosette said. "The styles I prefer always seem to go against what people expect of me."

"Exactly... The dresses I like are never the ones that suit me."

"Do you always end up going with the dress that suits you too?"

"Yes. I can avoid making a scene by wearing that one, so that's why I pick it."

"I completely understand..."

Regardless of how greatly they diverged from the impressions others had of them, they could never escape such tight molds. One girl was a pure, neat lily, and the other was a bewitching, gorgeous rose; praise that would be hard to bear at all, had there not been a grain of truth to them. These two walked the same path, so the troubles they faced and the hurdles that obstructed them were identical. Struggles like these couldn't be discussed with others, so now that each girl had found a sympathetic ear, it was as though the floodgates had opened up.

Rosette looked off into the distance, smiling. "It makes me happy to hear that light colors suit me, but I end up taking such pains to avoid dirtying them that I get a thousand times more tired out when I wear them."

Violette offered a wry smile of her own. "Stains do stand out more on light fabric..."

It was a refreshing exchange, and it lightened her mood. She could never have had a conversation like this with anyone else. Back when she was in middle school and soon after she advanced to high school, Violette was surrounded by a plethora of people.

She wondered how much of an uproar she would create if she spoke like this around them. Anyone who shattered their public image would be eaten alive by their former admirers. Those who pictured Violette as a queen who sat at the apex would never permit her to show the slightest hint of weakness.

In the past, that feeling had comforted her—immersing herself in a dream of being all-powerful helped her to feel strong in the real world. It dawned on her now how pressured she must have been to believe that. Once Violette herself had bought into the fantasy, rather than just those around her, it wasn't long before she abused her alleged power...though now wasn't the time to discuss that dark potential past. Nor did she have the time to waste wallowing in shame. How she wished that she could expunge all traces of that miserable history from her memory!

"I'm the opposite," she said. "Light colors don't suit me, so I don't have to worry about that...but don't you find the corsets to be painfully restrictive?"

What people demanded of Violette was elegant splendor and sensuality, for her presence alone to demand attention. Such impressions rarely endeared her to others, but endearing was the last thing they wanted her to be. The public wanted her to command attention while remaining at arm's length, which suited her needs; though she loathed standing out, it was preferable to the ire she'd receive were she to dress in bland, mousy attire.

She had never liked her appearance. If anything, she hated it. She had refused to take so much as look in a mirror in the past. Back then, she had despised every speck of what composed her, from the blood in her veins to her very genes. She wondered now when her features had become "normal" to her. She thought of the face she hated, her annoying hair, the detestable dresses that covered her body. Why had it all stopped feeling so unbearable?

It was because...Yulan complimented me.

What came to mind was the boy always smiling by her side. No matter what she wore—boy's clothes, dresses to accompany her haphazardly trimmed hair, even her favorite clothes that others scorned—he praised her with a broad smile that washed away everyone else's voices. Not once had he turned up his nose, regardless of who shot her dirty looks or how far her outfit strayed from the norm.

"It's beautiful. No, adorable. It really suits you."

"Everything you wear is wonderful, Vio."

His words let her take pride in herself, to recognize her body as her own. She didn't like a single thing about herself, be it her hair, her eyes, her blood, or even the cells that formed all those parts. She had begun to think that it was fine anyway. Yulan loved and treasured the parts of her that she detested. If he loved her, perhaps she could love herself through him.

"Er, Lady Violette?" Rosette called out.

"Urk! I-I'm sorry. I ended up...getting lost in a memory."

"Please, don't worry. Was it a nice one?"

"Huh?"

"Hee hee. Your face told the whole story. You looked delighted."

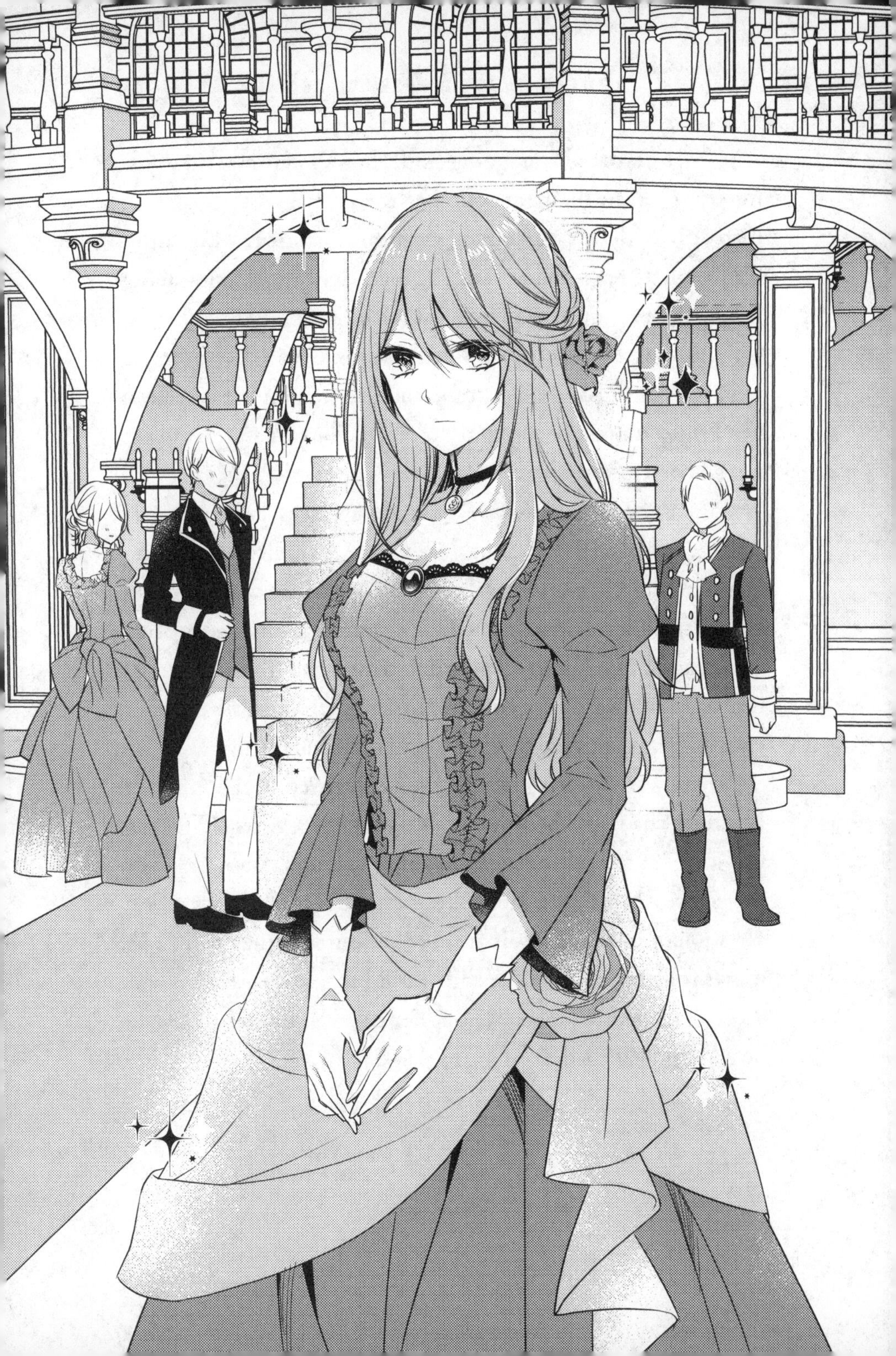

Rosette wore an easygoing smile, but Violette was at a loss for words. Even the faint sound of the breeze grew distant, so that only Rosette's voice rang clear and distinct in her mind. Had Violette really made such a happy face while thinking about Yulan? Even though the memory was hardly a pleasant one?

This world had warped Violette into a twisted, miserable criminal who wished misfortune and death upon those around her. Ethics, morals, and even the law could be cast aside. And yet, not all her memories were ugly.

"Yes..." she uttered slowly, "I *was* happy. I was...so happy."

She managed to force out these words, as riddled with pauses and trembling, silent intervals as they were. They were, without a doubt, Violette's true thoughts. Rosette was understandably concerned when Violette looked downward, both hands covering her face. It was all she could do to gently stroke Violette's back, even as the girl seemed to teeter on the verge of crying.

There were no tears in Violette's eyes. Even in the midst of her inner chaos and bafflement, all she could register right then was joy. She felt positively spoiled by Rosette's kindness, since the princess had accompanied her without asking any questions.

Violette *was* happy. That was the source of her pain. She wasn't fully aware of it; she hadn't tried to see what lay beyond. Violette longed to be happy...but her true happiness had always been right by her side, smiling for her.

84 The Ideal Person

VIOLETTE KEPT HER HEAD held low until the class bell rang, but Rosette didn't pry. She only asked if Violette was okay, expecting nothing back from Violette but a "sorry" or perhaps an "I'm fine." Then Rosette would reassure her in turn with a warm smile. The girl apparently knew the line between kindness and imposition well. Forcing past barriers might prove effective for certain people in crisis, but seeing as Violette couldn't verbalize her own needs, she was grateful for Rosette's restraint.

"I'm sorry, Lady Rosette," Violette said.

Today was the first day Violette had ever had an honest conversation, and she ended up letting her true feelings show on her face. Such a slipup would have been unthinkable for her normally. Though her budding feelings toward Yulan were a factor, she suspected the main reason was how similar her situation had been to Rosette's—far more similar than she could ever have imagined. Her heart had reacted to the comfort and camaraderie she felt with Rosette by opening up much too wide.

Violette and Rosette were both part of the unlucky few who faced equal pressure in both reality and the idealized world. Still, one mustn't assume that everyone in this minority perfectly understood one another. That would make them no different from the hopefuls who projected their ideals onto Rosette.

"I must have given you quite a shock," Violette muttered. "Please forget about it."

"No need to worry. Besides, I was the one who surprised *you* yesterday. We're equal now."

Violette thought there was a significant difference between discovering an inner secret that clashed severely with one's image and a sudden outburst of emotion, but Rosette did seem sympathetic. She couldn't tell if the princess was sincere about considering them equals or merely acting out of consideration for her well-being, but one thing was clear from this short exchange: Rosette's kindness. She didn't ridicule Violette, scrunch her face up in annoyance, or badger her for details, nor did she reprimand her. Violette was pleased to have been given this space just to *be*.

"Shall we head back for now? The class bell has already rung once, so I doubt we have much time left," Rosette said.

If they didn't return before the second bell rang, they would be late. Both the ill-favored Violette and the dearly beloved Rosette wanted to avoid that at all costs. The academy would send out an excessively large search party on the occasion that a student disappeared. It was to be expected, as the sons and daughters of the nobility and the royal family attended this school; however, it felt suffocating to the students themselves to cause such an uproar.

The walk back to the classrooms was essentially the same for all students. All of them were clustered together in the same corner of the campus, even if they were on separate floors. Nevertheless, even a single corner of this expansively large academy was frighteningly large. As she walked side by side with Rosette, Violette brought up something that had been on her mind.

"That reminds me," she began. "You knew where my class was."

All these surprises had eclipsed the fact, but she was curious as to how someone she'd never formally met had known which class she was in. Violette barely knew her own classmates' names. Obviously she wasn't in the same class as Rosette, but it shouldn't have mattered to the princess where she was if she had no clue where to start looking.

"All I heard was that you were in the next class over. You are, um...famous, after all."

Though she said it sweetly, Rosette was clearly referring to Violette's infamy. She had caused trouble for Claudia, and there had been a clamor after the matter with her half sister. Rosette was most likely referring to the latter. The former was Violette's own fault, of course, but she was forcibly dragged into the business with Maryjune. She didn't know whether to be angry or astonished that her father's interferences had an impact as far away as the academy, but settled for astonishment. Anger would only lead to the bad ending she'd endured in the past. It wasn't worth the energy.

"I couldn't tell which of the neighboring classes you were in, though. I intended to peer inside each of them." With an adorably bashful smile, she added, "Luckily, I guessed right the first time."

From the way she walked to the faces she made, Rosette personified elegance. It made sense that others lauded her as the ideal lady; Violette assumed she had mastered the mimicry of that ideal so thoroughly that it was second nature to her now. Rosette may have believed she was far from ideal, but her true nature was that of a lovely and respectable princess.

"It's my turn to track down your classroom, then," Violette said.

"Huh?"

"Yes... How does lunch sound?"

"Oh! A-absolutely! I'll be waiting for you!"

There was only one class next to Violette's, so she needn't go searching, as Rosette had done. Rosette had seen through her indirect invitation and readily agreed to it with bright pink cheeks and an ecstatic nod.

It was astonishing how quickly her refined image changed to one of childish innocence. Her expressions were so swift and clear that it was easy to read her mind, and though she wasn't able to speak freely, she felt her emotions with all of her heart. She was no softly smiling, passive listener. She actively took part in conversations like this. Flawless conduct aside, this Rosette was poles apart from her rumored image.

Knowing this about her wasn't necessarily a good thing. Violette wondered if it would have been better to remain ignorant of someone like Rosette, tormented by a secret yet able to conduct herself with grace. Confiding in someone didn't guarantee that things would get better from then on, and someone confessing a secret was no proof that they were trustworthy.

She knew that, but it changed nothing. Violette thought that Rosette looked beautiful yesterday, today, and even at this moment. With her former sophisticated impression laying in shards around her, this version of Rosette was everything Violette aspired toward.

I Swear I Won't Bother You AGAIN!

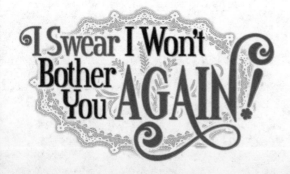

85 Such a Pretty Lie

"YOU DON'T EAT MUCH, do you, Lady Violette?" Rosette remarked.

"You think? I eat quite a lot of dessert."

The whole cafeteria may as well have frozen over. The reason was obvious: two of the most famous students, total opposites of one another, were sitting together to eat. Had she chosen corner seats in a fruitless bid to avoid the relentless staring, or had Rosette? They had each sensed it in the air, so it could have been either of them.

Sitting across from each other wasn't being received well, judging by all the whispers and suspicious looks. The students' suspicions toward Violette were surely reinforced by this arrangement. She wasn't one to care, but Rosette responded by kicking her smile up a notch as soon as they'd entered the cafeteria. Anyone would assume she was truly enjoying herself.

"Not a fan of sweets?" Violette asked.

Unlike Violette, whose dessert platter dwarfed her entrée, Rosette hadn't ordered anything sweet to go with her lunch.

While it was rare to see someone as head-over-heels for dessert as Violette, it wasn't common for students to skip dessert altogether.

Rosette replied in a hushed voice, "I don't hate them, but I prefer bitter foods." They both spoke quietly out of consideration for her public image.

The pair were simultaneously similar and dissimilar. The real Rosette was closer to the impression others held of Violette. Things may have been easier, in a sense, if they switched bodies... but all sorts of other problems would arise from that. It was just as well that it was an impossible solution.

"I see that you certainly enjoy them, though."

"I do. Conversely, I cannot handle bitter food no matter how I try."

"A shame. There are some delicious bitter dishes out there."

"You know, I thought I would be able to drink black coffee when I grew up."

"I understand. It's common to make baseless assumptions like those when you're young, right?"

"It's almost as though...you're attracted to the bitterness itself, I suppose? I fantasized about ordering a black coffee at a café and such."

"Think your fantasy will come true?"

"Not at *all*."

The two ladies emanated a sacred allure as they giggled together. Curious gazes were directed their way, but they weren't able to disturb the atmosphere between them—no onlookers dared to even consider it. None had the right to intrude on such a splendid, perfect scene.

"Coffee can taste completely different depending on the shop. Maybe you've got to find the right one?"

"That may be the issue. I can't say I frequent such places."

In the cafés with delicious sweets and cake shops with adorable displays, she was never really concerned about her inability to drink coffee.

All those places...I only knew about them because Yulan told me.

Her love for sweets only became public knowledge in her dark past, after her time in prison. That was how carefully she crafted her impression. Violette had maintained the facade of a strong, noble, and beautiful person for all this time, but before she noticed, that facade had distorted her into an oppressive and haughty creature. Now expected to enjoy black coffee to match that stern image, not sweets, she had learned to mimic pleasure at the bitterness that spread through her mouth.

Yulan would always secretly give me chocolates and marshmallows.

During parties, she would begrudgingly eat things only others approved of. Before she reached her limit, Yulan would sneak her some sweets, which allowed her to recover. Whenever she was tired and ran away to a deserted area, he would find her and present her with a mountain of sweets. His expression back then was in a state of permanent conflict; surely the sadness on his smiling face was real.

I must have worried him.

Violette hadn't realized it at all back then; this sudden epiphany must have come about because of her selfish desire to hoard him. Though she was glad to be reminded of how much she owed to Yulan, she also felt that she was strangling herself. She knew it would be better to stay away from him, but it was growing more and more difficult to do so.

She wanted to repay him for his kindness, but putting it like that felt inadequate. It was more that she needed to prove how deeply intense her gratitude was...but no, that fell short of describing her emotions too.

She knew better than anyone else what a wonderful person Yulan had become. He would be happy no matter who his partner was. What a pretty lie she'd told, wishing to stand nearby as an observer. Lip service. A flat-out lie. She wanted to smile next to, beside, and at the closest spot to him. She wanted him to smile at her. She wanted to make him happy.

If only the person Yulan loved was her...

"Huh?" Violette uttered.

A loud clatter rang out as her fork fell on the table.

"A-are you all right, Lady Violette?" Rosette asked.

"I-I'm sorry. I'm fine."

Panicking a little, Rosette summoned a waiter and asked for a new fork. Violette saw the scene before her, heard Rosette's concerned voice, and managed to respond. Her head, however, was wholly preoccupied by something else. Her cheeks grew warm, and her eyes welled with tears. Her hair shielded her downcast expression, and she was relieved for that small mercy. She must have looked pathetic.

She kept her lips from trembling, desperate to hold back all the emotions threatening to overflow.

Spiraling as she was, she could only manage desperate, fractured thoughts.

Just now, I...I—

What had she envisioned inside her own head just now?

I Swear I Won't Bother You AGAIN!

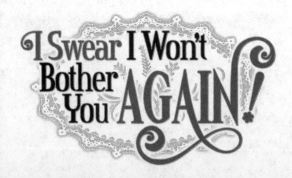

86 Asking for the Impossible

I T WAS OBVIOUS from the beginning that this feeling was
pure ego and nothing more.

❧

"You look grumpy," Gia commented.

Yulan didn't reply. He was acutely aware of the turbulent
aura emanating from him. It was so effective at putting people
off that one could easily assume he was doing it on purpose, but
such tactics weren't necessary. The typical aura around Yulan was
overwhelming; he hadn't had an entourage around him for some
time. More likely was that Yulan's classmates couldn't sense his
mood at all and perceived him as being deep in thought on some
topic. He didn't care whether they approached.

His friend completely disregarded the others' reactions,
though, so Yulan was driven to say something.

"Shut up, Gia," he growled.

"Hey, I said like three words!"

"Three words too many."

"Got an ego on you today, huh?"

Seeing Gia say it with a smile irritated Yulan even more. Had he even noticed Yulan's displeasure? It was just as likely that he had and had chosen to ignore it, even disregarded it as something not worth addressing. Yulan's foul moods barely seemed to register to Gia as worthy of concern. To Yulan, who calculated his relationships based on their worth, Gia was easy to deal with: an outside observer who was free to engage with Yulan and others on his own terms. It was something that Yulan appreciated about him, but it also meant that he had to keep Gia at a certain amount of distance.

Gia neither offered blunt advice in the proclamation of his sense of justice nor donned the mask of a supporter to offer counsel that suited his own agenda. He created a clear divide between himself and others. He wouldn't notice if hell itself rose up around him, provided he was in a face-to-face conversation with someone. Yulan could be completely frank with him. Talking to the foreign prince did, however, stir up other emotions in him.

Many of the other students detested Gia, the exotic imperial prince who was confined in this country under the pretense of neutrality. Yulan, by contrast, was saddled with far knottier personal circumstances than Gia. His attractive appearance, expression, and personality allowed him to fit in despite it. Yulan had planned and engineered that outcome himself, using expert cunning and intelligence to earn the adoration of the students around him. Yet Gia lived without a care, showing indifference, freedom, and extraordinary strength.

Wild horses couldn't draw the truth from Yulan's lips: he was jealous of that freedom. Jealous and resentful of it.

"I told you to shut up, already. You're giving me a headache."

"Aah. Didn't sleep well? You've got dark circles."

"I'm aware."

Yulan had all sorts of things to think about, and he was getting half the amount of sleep he usually got. This, combined with his naturally low blood pressure, made his mood foul and his health shoddy. He hadn't intended to lapse in his self-care, but his worries had left him little time to prioritize it.

I just can't gather enough info here.

He had been scrutinizing what limited information he had, analyzing it, and investigating credible threads. Nevertheless, the cards he had in his hand were hardly any different from before; his efforts hadn't borne fruit. Pushing himself to the point of restless nights had been a waste, but he didn't have the option to stop.

I wonder if Vio's all right.

Violette's expression the last time he saw her played back in his mind. He saw again her face composed of surprise, panic, and despair, and her back as she left right after. The scene played back over and over, making him hate the cause of it all even more. He had a general idea of where the blame might lie, but that made it all the more aggravating that he didn't know any concrete facts.

As he rubbed his aching temples to stimulate them, he yearned to place the blame on her bothersome younger sister.

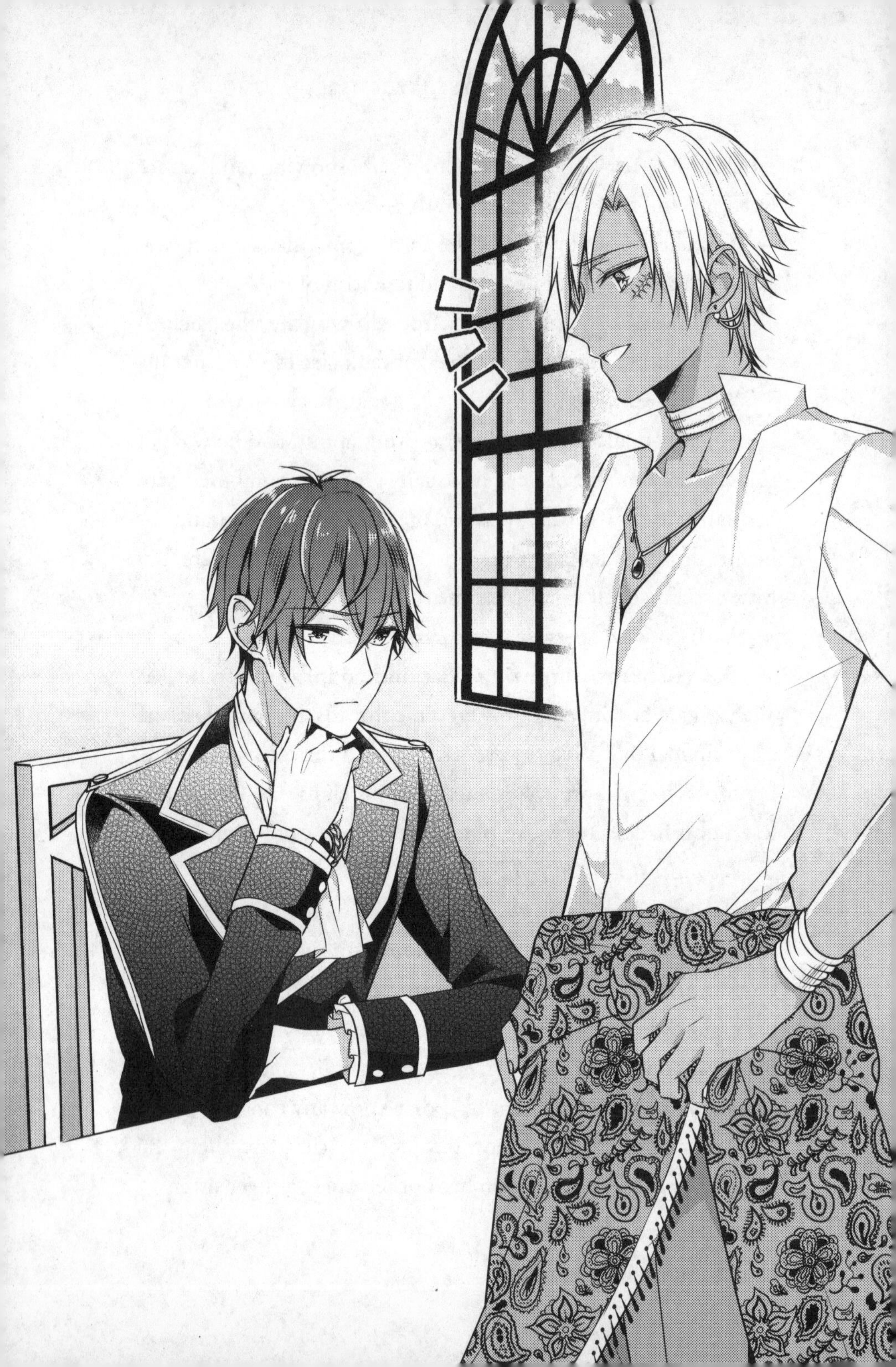

As I thought, I'd better find out what's been going on at her house.

Asking Violette herself was out of the question. Yulan wouldn't dare remind her of home when she wasn't anywhere near it. Besides, she probably wouldn't tell him anything. She had tried to deceive him with a smile and an "I'm fine" numerous times. He should have realized sooner that this wasn't an admission of calm but a front of endurance.

It would be best to ask Miss Marin, but...

Marin understood Violette like he did. Violette undoubtedly trusted her maid more than anyone else in the world. If Yulan could get in contact with her, not only would his questions be resolved, but he could also gain other information. The problem was the level of risk involved.

Firstly, he had no way of personally contacting Marin. She was a servant, so there was practically no way to contact her without using an intermediary. He could try calling the Vahan household, but Marin may not be the one to answer him. If he sent her a letter, he wouldn't know who would be around to see it.

Had the duke still been living in another residence and Bellerose shuttered away in her room, Yulan would've had an avenue to reach out—back then, all the servants were sympathetic to Violette. Now, however, there were three foreign agents in the house, each with their own servants in tow. Those servants' allegiances might lie elsewhere. Yulan trusted Marin, but that trust did not extend toward anyone else in the household.

"Tch."

Was this a stalemate? No, things weren't so dire yet. He needed moves to play, that was it. There was a plethora of things to think about. Still, he would need to come up with a way to contact Marin as a last resort. This conundrum was worsening his sleep faster than he could fix it.

"Sorry to butt in on your navel-gazing sesh, but there's this one thing I wanted to tell you."

Yulan hadn't realized his gaze was lowered until he looked up at Gia, who had casually taken the seat in front of him. The glare he shot his friend was unintentional; his headache was to blame. "What?"

Gia wasn't shaken by the sharp look, such a drastic turn from Yulan's typical lost-kitten countenance. He parted his thin lips to ask a nonchalant question:

"D'you know of Rosette Megan?"

87   "Princess," Defined

"**S**HE'S THE 'NOBLE PRINCESS,' right? What about her?" Yulan asked.

Rosette Megan was the epitome of a picture-perfect princess. Her reputation had grown more inflated over time until she was synonymous with the concept. Many of the academy's students eyed her with envy. Gia, a fellow international student, received the opposite response, but it all came down to appearances.

The princess had the same fair skin as the people of Duralia and hair representative of the kingdom of Lithos, whereas the brash prince was loud and differed in both his looks and attitude. Yulan thought the people who judged them differently were stupid, but it made them easy for him to understand. Once he had matured and could smile beautifully, he easily deceived everyone around him—despite having the most hated golden eyes in the country. These same people would justify Yulan's existence by claiming that it wasn't the outside but the inside that mattered. They would never even imagine that Yulan was only an empty husk.

"So you know her, then," Gia replied.

"I know her name, at least. She's famous."

"Yeah, I guess she must be. Enough that I know her."

"You two are in the same social class, no?"

"Nah. My people are a whole other kettle of fish."

"Right."

Gia's home country, as seen from a foreigner's point of view, was too challenging to understand. Upon studying abroad, Gia himself had realized that what he considered commonplace seemed strange to outsiders.

"So, what's this about Princess Rosette?" Yulan asked. He threw Gia a look that said, "If it's something stupid, I'll knock you out."

Gia clenched his teeth to hold back his laughter. He knew well that if he let it out, his friend would explode. He wasn't sure whether Yulan's poor mood was caused by his lack of sleep or something else, but whatever it was, he seemed five times more volatile than usual. His personality meant he'd probably hold himself back even if Gia was tactless, but he'd find perfectly targeted ways to make him regret it later.

Gia felt no small amount of trepidation about giving a guy like Yulan this information...but, to be honest, he was sure Yulan would see through him even if he kept his mouth shut.

"I saw her with *your* princess not too long ago."

"Go on."

"It wasn't like I was over there chatting with them, so I don't know any more than that, but...the two of 'em really stood out."

"I suppose they would."

Both ladies stood out in their own way, but one could easily imagine the fervor they'd attract while next to each other. That wasn't Yulan's concern, however.

Why were those two together?

They had no common ground, as far as he was aware. Their classes were next to each other, certainly, but that wasn't noteworthy: each grade only had three classes. He couldn't think of any mutual acquaintances they might have. Most importantly, the two girls were completely different. One was idolized, one was ostracized. Each drew a bevy of stares wherever they went.

Yulan could imagine several pretexts for the two to have been together since they were in the same grade. Gia may have caught nothing more than the two exchanging greetings, but there was no evidence to prove or deny that fact. Without proof, any hypotheticals he drew up were exactly that—neither truth nor lie.

"Do you know where they went?" Yulan asked.

"Uh, lemme think. They were heading over to the courtyard, I guess...?"

"I see."

"You heading there now?"

"You assumed I would when I told you, didn't you?"

"Make sure you're back before class starts."

Yulan had already left the room before Gia was done talking. His information network was vast enough that he could pinpoint the ladies' location based on those meager details, and it was especially easy to track down someone who stood out. Once he arrived, he would watch over the girl from afar. Naturally, he was referring to Violette.

"I wonder where the other princess fits into all this," Gia murmured to himself.

The "Noble Princess" in Gia's memory beamed with an intensity far beyond her typical elegant smiles.

"If you take that kid for nothing more than a 'princess,' you'll be the one who ends up paying for it."

88 A Fragment of Unease

Violette was completely bereft after what had happened. She left over half of her lunch untouched and even abandoned the dessert she was so eager to taste. Her behavior was suspicious, even unstable. Rosette was worried for her, no matter how Violette protested that she was fine.

Rosette had only engaged in a brief exchange with Violette, but even she noticed that her words didn't reflect her true feelings. Since Violette remained unable to put her feelings into words, both were stuck holding surface-level conversations while Rosette averted her gaze. Violette tried to process her emotions and the reality thrust upon her.

Perhaps for the first time in her life, Violette saw the benefits to having a family who didn't care about her. Whenever she was in pain, having a hard time, or worried, they would leave her alone. Her gratitude had a limit, mind you, because her family's absurd number of drawbacks far outweighed the advantages. She thought this preferable to having her insecurity crushed into a fine powder, but then again, she didn't have much choice in the matter.

Her family wouldn't notice her panicked state when she returned home, nor would they visit her if she stayed cooped up in her room. She was relieved that Maryjune wasn't home yet; the girl would undoubtedly pick up on her abnormal state and corner her if she were present.

"Welcome home, Lady Violette," Marin said.

Violette entered her room as Marin was cleaning up. Upon seeing her mistress close the door behind her with her gaze to the floor, Marin shot her a suspicious look. Violette appeared to have returned home earlier than normal, but her movements were sluggish and unsteady. Though the sight of Violette brimming with energy in this house would be most unnerving, she was clearly depressed beyond the norm. She would normally suppress her emotions in a far more adroit manner than this, enduring until her last nerve gave out.

"Did something—"

Marin intended to finish her question with "happen?" but her view was suddenly enveloped in gray. The sheets in Marin's arms fluttered down to the floor as Violette clung to her, savoring the warmth of her body. Violette buried her face in Marin's shoulder and wrapped both arms around her back, presumably wrinkling her maid uniform as she did so.

The maid was wholly taken aback by the gesture. She promptly caught her mistress, but she had no idea what to do next. Marin simply looked down at the head slightly shorter than her own and stiffened. Marin was so confused that she couldn't even conceive of wrapping her own arms around Violette's back.

"Lady Violette...?" Marin asked.

Violette had never held on to her like this before. They had touched before: as she took care of Violette, Marin endeavored to heal her heart, to dote on and console her, and physical touch was a way to do so. Similarly, Violette had caressed Marin's hair and cheeks with her dainty hand. She expressed her gratitude that way and also comforted the hardworking maid whose heart ached for her sake. They had certainly never gotten this close before, however... They couldn't have.

Marin wished she could hug Violette forever, warming her up and letting her cry into her chest. She didn't want Violette to be terrorized by nightmares or hug herself to sleep. How happy Marin would have been to share her warmth with this cold and fragile body. She had wished fervently that she'd be given the chance to protect Violette with her own arms.

But of course, I...I couldn't...

Marin was afraid of hugging Violette back. Marin recalled the image of *that* woman smiling and hugging Violette when she was a child. The girl sat dull and lifeless as a corpse in the woman's ecstatic embrace. The mother's every utterance robbed yet more vitality from her daughter, spewing poison from her lips in the form of love. Her repugnant, shining eyes—the same red color as Marin's—only compounded the nightmare.

I couldn't bear to take on the image of that...thing.

Marin's eyes were similar to Bellerose's, and Violette herself called them beautiful. Those words had changed Marin's life, and from then on, she kept a safe home for Violette in the depths of her heart.

So...that fear was what was stopping me, was it?

As that tiny seed sprouted and bloomed, another emotion took root within her. The more Marin cherished Violette, the more anxious she felt about the red hue she had, at last, grown fond of. The horrible scene from that day refused to leave her mind. With limp arms, unfocused eyes, and an emotionless voice, Violette had clearly renounced living back then. If Marin were to embrace Violette, and her name were called with such an expression, in such a voice... Imagining it made Marin's heart feel like it was being torn to shreds.

Marin slowly placed her hands on Violette's back. Her fingers curled into the strands of hair that she had just touched this morning. When she traced the strands to confirm their softness, she felt the warmth of life radiating from Violette's entire body. This person was unmistakably alive. Her beloved mistress was still breathing, even inside her arms.

Immediately, Marin's suffocating anxiety was washed away. What she'd seen as a wall between them had really just been mist. She wasn't being held back; she merely hadn't been able to step forward. Her mind had conjured up an illusion that had no relation to what Violette actually felt. In this moment, Violette was clinging to her. Violette was brimming with emotion, yearning for something, and right now, she needed Marin. There was only one thing for Marin to do in such a situation.

"What is the matter, Lady Violette?"

I Swear I Won't Bother You AGAIN!

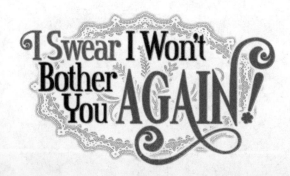

89 Calling Out the Lie

MARIN'S VOICE CAME DOWN from above like a warm blanket. The hand stroking Violette's back was comfortably soft and rhythmic, and soothed her like a child being lulled to sleep. Marin's temperature ran cool compared to most people, but it felt warm to Violette's cold body. Violette pressed her forehead against the maid's shoulder as she brooded over how she could possibly shape these disorganized thoughts into speech. Each time she opened her mouth, only breath came out. Perhaps that was just as well. If she were able to speak, the best she could offer was an outline of what had really happened.

"M-Marin... I...I'm..."

Violette's tongue failed her. Some dam had broken inside her head, and she needed to cling onto her maid lest she collapse. She was letting her emotions take control, but she didn't know what else to do. Should she cry her eyes out? Should she give whatever unsatisfying explanation she could manage, then seek counsel for it? Should she allow her emotions to gush out of her, messy and raw, in the hope that Marin would validate them and lighten her burden?

Surely, past Violette would have taken the third option. Her lone comfort was her belief that she was the heroine of a tragedy. As long as someone agreed to be her ally, that was enough—she cared not whether they did so out of sympathy or pity. What she wanted was grounds to convince herself of being in the right.

Here and now, however, she wanted something else entirely.

"Lady Violette, calm down. Take it slowly and—"

"N-no. It's all...wrong!"

Although Marin tried to meet Violette's gaze to reassure her, Violette's unblinking eyes darted from one direction to another in blatant panic. Her head felt as hot as though her brain were boiling; she felt its heat simmer the backs of her eyes. While her body burned, her hands and heart steadily froze. She was simultaneously heating up and cooling down. Burning and freezing. Her emotions and reasoning, which should have informed her true feelings, were now screaming at each other from opposite sides. If only one of the two were false! Then she could single it out, tear her emotions or logic out from within herself. Alas, it was all true. She couldn't bear it.

"I...I've...fallen in love with Yulan!"

Inside, she howled that it was impossible, a delusion, and a dream created by her desire to monopolize him. She pleaded for someone, anyone, to disprove her.

"It's wrong. All of it, it's...wrong. It can't be..."

Violette was supposed to beg for love, to hunger and to thirst for it. All the love stories that built up around Violette had tragic endings. Her feelings for Claudia weren't love: he represented a stepping stone to happiness that lay beyond him, but she didn't necessarily wish for his affection specifically. She wanted to be loved by many people. Anyone would do and their love could come in any form, no matter how twisted or polluted. Violette would accept any and all of those feelings with a welcome heart. Assuming that the opposite of love was disinterest, to Violette, any interest at all could be interpreted as love.

The only love she'd ever known was deep, dark, and heavy as lead. It compelled you to devote your life, or even that of your own child, to a single person. This was a desire that took in the tears shed around it as sustenance to make it bloom. Bellerose's face had shone with desire...and on her deathbed, it was tarnished with equal shares of disappointment, despair, hatred, and disgust. This was what love looked like through Violette's eyes.

"No, I don't... Ngh! I don't want it to be like this!"

Bellerose would crow Auld's name as she cradled Violette's cheeks with both hands. Was it fortune or misfortune that Violette hadn't developed the ego to assert herself back then, before her brain could do little more than recognize words? She recalled one thing to this day, even so: the terror held in those glittering eyes, the color of fresh blood.

The training Violette had been subjected to was somehow both harsh and indulgent. Bellerose was awfully strict when it came to doing things exactly as her father had but remained unconcerned however poorly Violette performed as a lady in society. Even if Violette were to run around outside or climb trees, Bellerose cheerfully permitted it as long as Violette didn't get injured or suntanned. Bellerose seemed to have no issue with her daughter's boyish behavior. Rather, her discomfort lay in her daughter's burgeoning womanhood. The more feminine Violette became, the more likely her mother would discard her as a poor substitute for her father.

Bellerose viewed Violette as a sacrifice for her love, an offering that she had birthed herself. Unfortunately, her father refused her gift, and it was then that Bellerose found an even more valuable—and terrible—role for Violette to perform. In the depths of insanity, she fashioned her daughter into a failed imitation of her beloved, all in the hope of an earnest sign of affection.

This proved that the emotion flooding Violette's heart could not be love. It would be too awful to bear if it were.

So then, why...?

"Why? Why do I feel so happy?" Violette whispered.

This emotion was precious to her now. It was valuable enough to her that it brought her to the verge of tears. And yet she pleaded to herself that it could not, could never, be love.

90 Blue Tweedia

VIOLETTE'S DESIRE SURGED, receded, and then surged forth once more. As much as she believed it would suffocate her if left to thrive, she couldn't bear to kill it off. Its seeds must have been sown a long time ago, somewhere secure in the innermost, inscrutable depths of her heart where even she could not reach. That was why she had never noticed, and before she had the chance, the seed shattered its confines and spread its roots all throughout her body. Her heart could conceal this feeling no longer.

She wanted someone to uproot it, by force if need be. Then she wanted someone to torch the land so nothing else could ever grow there again. That would help her wake up and realize that this happiness was all a delusion.

"Marin, I—"

"Lady Violette."

Violette looked desperate to be rescued from her terror. Her hand grasped for the maid again. Marin firmly gripped it and refused to let go. The warmth in the maid's assertive hand

and the tone calling her name made the lost child finally look into her sunset-colored eyes.

"It's fine," Marin said firmly.

Each word was vivid and clear, all the better for Violette to receive them. The aural vibrations carried those words, and their intent, to every last inch of her body.

"It's *fine*. There is nothing to be afraid of. You have no need to worry."

Marin's candid tone wasn't much different from usual. There was nothing special about these words, announced as a matter of fact, but it was unbelievably difficult for Violette to accept them. *How terrifying it is to be assured without evidence that everything is fine.*

"B-but, I... I-I..."

Violette's trembling lips couldn't filter her scattered thoughts. Adrift in the depths of her fear as she was, she felt that even agreeing with Marin's affirmation was a sin.

She had made a grave error before. Love, affection, fortune— all of it came at a dear cost, and she hadn't realized how dear that cost had been. Violette's so-called "first love" was riddled with a bracing number of missteps. She had cast countless people into misery, brought yet more to tears. It didn't bode well.

"I-If I hurt him," she gasped, struggling to stay afloat, "what should I do?"

The mere thought of it horrified her.

Marin recalled the time when Violette had told her about her love in perfect detail. With a delighted smile and in a high-pitched voice, Violette had gushed that she had found someone she loved. Bellerose had left the girl a hollow shell, so it was significant that the husk of Violette had regained her heart. One-sided illusion or not, no one could condemn her for dreaming of happiness, and Marin and Yulan in particular were the last people to say a word against her.

Stable though she was when talking about Claudia, there was something decidedly off about Violette's manner. Given that her feelings were hardly pure, it was to be expected; Violette's desperation to be loved was stoked ever higher by Claudia's refusal to yield. She seemed primed to explode at any moment...and Marin thought she likely *would*, until recently.

The gunpowder was dampened. The timer stopped. The dreaded bomb turned into a cluster of junk as though by magic.

"It's all right," Marin said again. She repeated it, again and again, to the girl caught in the throes of her own panic. Then, she abruptly changed tack. "Do you like me, Lady Violette?"

"Hm?" Violette hesitated. "O-of course. I love you."

"I also love you, Lady Violette."

Violette cocked her head in confusion. Marin answered her with a smile so faint that few would have recognized it as such.

"You have never hurt me. You have loved me in earnest."

Being lovers and being mistress and servant were two different things. Marin, who hadn't experienced love for herself, could nevertheless imagine that the nature of the relationship, the emotions involved, and even the significance of that love were all different. Still, Marin had known since long ago that Violette treasured her and that this was love. Much of the happiness in Marin's life had been generated from that love.

She understood Violette's fear all too well. The reality they had experienced and grown up in was a filthy one. Both she and Violette, exploited by reality, couldn't afford to believe in beautiful love stories. Violette's dream of a "first love"—a dream she yearned and struggled for, and finally seized—was an echo from her painful past, nothing more. Marin didn't want Violette to let go of her feelings over something so inconsequential.

"Please, don't be afraid. Do not throw away your love."

No longer able to stand, Violette shakily sat down on the floor. Marin would ordinarily escort Violette to the sofa at once, but instead, she also sat down and pressed her face against that of her mistress. The girl looked up at her like a young child, brow furrowed in unease, so Marin reassured her yet again that everything was fine.

"Please don't reject the idea that you can be happy."

Being on the verge of tears while expressing her feelings was far better than talking about her first love with a fake smile plastered on her face. As much as Marin wished to see Violette smile, this honesty was preferable. Marin would never allow any pain or hatred to inhibit Violette's happiness in the long term, and that was twice as true of Yulan.

"I'm so blessed to be loved by you," Marin told her.

From the day her life had been saved until now, Marin had received many blessings. It was completely different from her life

in the church, where her scant emotions ranged from disappointment to annoyance. Even though she harbored many negative
and indescribable feelings like pain and anger, none of them
would change how she felt right now. Loving Violette, and being
loved by her, made Marin happy.

"I was...happy," Violette admitted.

At last, Violette's stubborn feeling broke the surface. Her tiny
voice could only reach Marin, who sat but a hair's breadth away.
That was fine. Marin didn't want anyone else to hear. Violette's
true feelings were that precious, sacred, and delicate to her.

"When I realized it, I...was happy."

"Right."

"I mean, it's just... Yulan... He's so, so wonderful."

"Yes."

"He's kind. He...always smiles for me."

"Right."

"He would...always be with me, listening...to me talk."

"Mm-hmm."

"He'll call my name, call me Vio. His voice makes me feel so
warm inside."

Putting her feelings into words gave them flesh, blood, and
shape. His figure grew clear in her mind. She could picture her
beloved's broad form turning to look at her, his soft hair swaying
in the breeze.

"He told...me...that I...wasn't alone."

As Violette slowly closed her eyes, she could see Yulan smiling and saying thank you that day.

I Swear I Won't Bother You AGAIN!

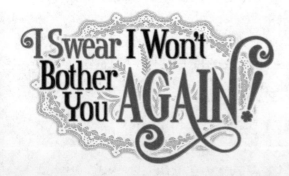

Side Story – The Foreign Prince, Part 1

A PRINCE FROM A FOREIGN COUNTRY—that was all he was.

❧

The moment that Gia was born into the Sina royal family, it was his fate to leave his country and study abroad. Gia came to the Tanzanite Academy around when he was due to enroll in middle school; his two older brothers had already returned from their time abroad by then, so his future was set in stone.

The other countries called their homeland "the Sina Empire," but to Gia and the other citizens, it didn't matter whether it was designated an empire, a kingdom, or whatever else you could call it. Sina was Sina.

Gia knew that outsiders disapproved of the Sinan way of thinking, dismissing it as shockingly frivolous and irresponsible. In fact, many visiting diplomats had turned tail and headed home as soon as they arrived. They claimed that while Sina housed much hidden potential, the nature of its citizens was impossible to bear for any length of time. As a prince from such a country, Gia could easily surmise how he would be received by the citizens of Duralia.

Although the prince had little interest in such affairs, members of the royal family were expected to have at least *some* sort of social life. He chose instead to ignore those who sought relations with his father, disregard the women his parents paired him with, and wholly devote himself to sating his appetite.

The moment his foot touched Duralian ground, he thought, *Jeez, this place is so stuffy and stifling. I can barely breathe.* The air here was much too different from the one in his homeland.

Here in Duralia, the king was a separate entity from his subjects, and it was everyone's duty to take that as fact. Those in the upper echelons were special; those at the bottom were common. Any given household of nobles was revered in an almost religious way by the Duralian populace, granted the honor earned by their forefathers. This was a country where order trumped freedom and reason was valued over instinct. "All for one, and one for all"— that is, kindness meant prioritizing others, and self-preservation equated to cowardice. The good of the group was universal justice.

This was the polar opposite of how things were in Sina.

Sina had established laws, but to comply with those laws was to prioritize instinct over reason, self over others, and group over the country. The law-abiding citizens of Sina were people who didn't care for others' opinions and only desired to walk the path they wanted to walk. They confused courage with recklessness and would risk their very lives for a burst of momentary pleasure.

This outlook was common in Sina but came off as disorderly and savage to outsiders. Worse, the outsider critics typically told the truth of what they witnessed within its borders...as impossible and fantastical some of their claims may have been.

Is this what my bros were talkin' about?

Gia recalled what his two older brothers had told him before he left to study abroad. Both had completed their own study programs, and as such, spoke from experience.

"You're gonna be fine...but you'd better not forget one thing. However sick you get of things over there, you ain't comin' back home," they'd said in their usual tone.

They weren't worried about their younger brother or that they wouldn't see him for a few years. Nor were they saddened by his departure. This was a simple, uncomplicated scene, a typical slice of their daily lives. Gia was still young when they left for their own study trips, and so he couldn't properly conceive of how long a few years truly were. Now that they had left their student days behind, they had a better grip on the span of time and could anticipate what lay in store for Gia.

Even family members held little interest in one another's affairs. It was one reason why people from other countries couldn't handle Sinan citizens; it was treated as a given that people would be curious about one another, and that went double for those raised in so-called respectable countries.

"Is that *him*?" a student whispered.

"He looks utterly uncivilized," murmured another. "Just like the rumors said."

People whispered as they stared at him. The students and sometimes adults would express displeasure at his appearance, behavior, and anything else about him they could, as if some dirty, wild animal had entered their line of sight.

His tan skin and silver hair were an indelible strike against his noble lineage. The casual way that Gia wore his beautiful, elegantly designed uniform made him stick out like a sore thumb from his surroundings; he couldn't help but attract stares. On the occasions that he did try to tame his roguish, natural good looks, he would unintentionally capture their attention and draw their fascination all the more.

That only intensified their distaste toward him, however. To these people, nothing was more disgraceful than to be compelled by someone they perceived as beneath them. Gia, for his part, refused to feel any culpability for how the masses felt. They were the ones who chose to hate him, to be fascinated by him, and to detest him at their own discretion. He found it rather rich that, in their arrogance, they labeled the citizens of Sina as outrageous barbarians. From his point of view, these people were far worse: self-centered, egotistical brats. If you didn't like someone, why bother getting involved with them? Why go out of your way to look at them? Better to forget about them entirely.

Manners, duty, compliments, and upholding appearances were nothing but a bother. Sinan people could live as they liked and die as they liked; in Sina, you were allowed to live by your own rules. Admittedly, that did make various aspects of life hard to handle, and as a result it was hardly discussed as an easy place to live—particularly in comparison to other countries. Ironically, it was an easier place to live than anywhere else in some regards—and especially for people who had their priorities straight. Especially for people like Gia.

"Well, whatever," Gia said to himself.

He let out a long yawn, opening his mouth wide. Such behavior was certain to prompt another wave of snide comments about his vulgarity, lack of manners, and unprincely conduct. It must be nice, he mused, having the luxury to waste so much time and emotion on other people's business.

To Gia, other people were just that: completely separate entities to himself. Regardless of whether they were family or friends, he didn't think they were the same as him. Love and passion weren't things to be shared among such people, but given and received. He wouldn't feel the same pain if someone he loved was injured. He could swear vengeance on their behalf, but they wouldn't suffer together in the same way.

He had a refreshing lack of interest in other people's affairs. His very emotions themselves were languid and lenient in how they progressed—for instance, instead of getting angry, he would feel less happy. Three seconds after professing a curiosity about something, he would lose interest altogether. There were times when he gratefully accepted a present only to forget about it and leave it behind.

Freer than the wind, lighter than feathers, Gia was beyond the understanding of even his parents and brothers. He was wild, selfish, bold, and lively—the very personification of Sina.

❧

Today, much like every other day, Gia was exiled from the tiny inner world of the academy. He'd chosen to act as though the exclusion didn't bother him one bit, and since then, he felt as though the social rejection had only grown worse with every passing day. People talked behind his back, pointedly ignored him, left him isolated, but no matter what tactics they tried his face showed no reaction. His composure further irritated those around him, as they felt he was implying that they must be petty and narrow-minded to focus on him to such an extent. In truth, Gia hadn't even given them that much consideration. Their spite continued to fester. With no way to stem their suspicions, they only continued to spread unabated—"concern for others" may have sounded like a pretty concept, full of goodwill, but here in this country it had a much darker side.

Gia's feelings weren't hurt. He barely had the capacity for such sensitivity in the first place. The gossip reaching his ears was grating, and it was inconvenient that he couldn't even hold the bare minimum of a conversation. But, well, that was all within his tolerance level. He didn't really care.

Welp, guess this is how things're gonna go.

In the cafeteria at lunchtime, he only concentrated on moving his mouth. *Chomp, chew, chomp, chew.* Everything he put into his mouth was extremely delicious, but he couldn't thoroughly enjoy the country's blessings because of the lifestyle of its citizens. Exhausting as he found it all, he had resigned himself to living this way. That was fine. All of it was fine by him. However, there was one much bigger problem that loomed large in his perspective.

There's nothin' goin' on here.

This place was boring, uninteresting, and dull. There was no pleasure. No enjoyment. No stimulation. No excitement.

I'm real tired of this.

What did he just swallow? What was he eating again? The act of consumption became an inconsequential process, and one that he took no delight in. He had no thoughts about this delicious meal besides it being nourishment. Three seconds prior, he'd thought that this was his only enjoyment in this boring country. When his focus failed, it had taken his appetite along with it.

The mountain of bread remained a mountain. His stomach wasn't full. The hand that brought more of it to his lips didn't stop. His jaws continued to chew. The problem was that he found it all too tiresome to bear. He stuffed the space in his stomach for the sake of stuffing it. He imagined Little Red Riding Hood had a similar rationale when she stuffed the wolf's stomach with stones. At last, he understood the meaning behind his brothers' warning.

How many more years of this?

It had only been several months since he enrolled. That left over five more years until he could graduate high school. Five more years before Gia could leave this country, without exception. No matter if a ceremonial occasion called for the whole royal family, or if he merely wished to visit home during a long vacation, Gia wouldn't be allowed to take a single step outside

Duralia until he graduated from the academy. The school's regulations—and Sina's law—expressly forbade it.

The kingdom of Duralia and Tanzanite Academy weren't generous enough to accept the Sina royal family from the outset. Likewise, Sina found little attractive about Duralia at all. The peace-advocating kingdom and the empire that swore by instinct clashed like water and oil; only a fool would think that they could coexist. The rule that prevented Sinan royal students at the academy from returning home was established explicitly because such frivolous people might otherwise abandon Duralia for their own shores with no warning.

Gia was a student, but the only areas outside the academy that he could visit were ones where he didn't need to prove his citizenship. Forget going back to his own country an ocean away, he wasn't allowed to get anywhere near it. Granted, he had never tried, but why bother? He knew he'd be taken back in a matter of seconds. This country's peace was in part due to its importance to their national identity, yes—but it owed just as much to their excellent security. If, perchance, he were to discover a secret passage back to his country, all he expected to find at the end was an order for execution by decapitation on account of treason.

It mattered little whether he stayed here or ran away back home. Boredom would be the death of him, either way.

I'm amazed my bros put up with this. Doubt I'll make it, to be honest.

He wanted something, anything, to pique his interest. Something fun. Anything or anyone would be fine, as long as it could vanquish this boredom. Some stimulation. Some excitement. He wanted a toy that could keep him entertained.

Just then, he heard someone's voice.

"You're going to eat all that?"

I Swear I Won't Bother You AGAIN!

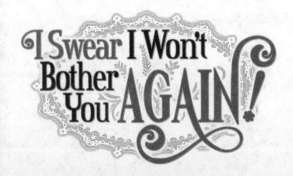

Side Story - The Foreign Prince, Part 2

AN EXPRESSIONLESS SMILE—such a contradiction suited this boy all too well.

❧

Sina was an island rolling in profits and brimming with animosity, but no one could tell how it came to be like that. Though it was referred to as an "empire," no one knew much about its inner workings. When Yulan tried to investigate, he found no Sinan natives, let alone anyone with any real knowledge of how the nation operated. People only knew shallow bits of information: its name, its location, and so on.

Allegedly, Sinan people chose instinct over reason, excitement over security, and stimulation over tranquility. They had no intelligence or character, and in fact were closer to beasts than humans. They weren't a country but a mob. Everyone looked down on them. However, Yulan was neither naive nor foolish enough to take such rumors for fact.

Duralia was a country that respected peace and benevolence. The aristocratic world kept the country functioning, but prying away its lid revealed a quagmire of irony and scorn. While these so-called beasts were unaware of their potential to be clever, they at least recognized how little they knew. Ignorance was shameful, but failing to acknowledge the depths of your own ignorance was far worse. In Yulan's opinion, such ignorance was not only shameful but dangerous too.

When he was young, Yulan didn't have the luxury of the protective shield given to other children. Instead, he walked naked and bare through a torrent of human malice. As he advanced, covered in wounds, he craved any kind of weapon. A lance would have been wonderful, but a shield would do; he could swing it wildly without a care, use its blunt force to stave away anything in his way.

Thinking back on it, he was glad that his wishes went unfulfilled. If he had gone on such a rampage in his younger days, he wouldn't be where he was today. He would have never met Violette or known of her pain. He would have burned himself out without knowing her voice or her face, and then he would have spent his life from the cradle to the grave without an ounce of purpose. Fortunately, Yulan did encounter Violette, and she healed all his wounds from the painful journey he'd undergone in his youth.

Now he sought strength, not for his own sake, but to better shield Violette. He trained his body, improved his physique, and honed his mind, but even after all that, he felt lacking. Scraping together a laundry list of the necessary qualities wouldn't suffice; he had to learn how to curate his skills, to know how best to apply them.

He'd started his investigation on Sina during his attempts to brush up on geography and world history but never uncovered anything more in-depth than a three-line summary. Even though he assumed he should be able to research it to the same degree as all the other countries he studied, Sina alone remained a mystery.

Right as Yulan was on the verge of giving up on learning about Sina, he heard about Gia Forte.

It was hardly a strange phenomenon for Sinan royalty to enroll in the academy. However, the majority of the students had no knowledge of the Sinan prince's age, and therefore they hadn't anticipated his arrival. This made it all the more easier for them to reject the foreign prince as if he were an alien who appeared out of nowhere.

Thrown into a crowd of peers too immature to understand how great a privilege it was to be protected, Gia was constantly gossiped about and even occasionally harmed. Most people around him were so absorbed in their own blithe, peaceful school days that they couldn't comprehend the effects their actions had on him. After all, the prince looked different to them. The circumstances of his birth were different, and he held different views. Crowds of people in Duralia advocated for individuality, yet those same people couldn't bear how he differed from them. An open mind and a high tolerance level might initially sound similar, but there was a crucial disparity between them. Their tolerance for such things could wear thin or run out altogether in certain situations. And when everyone gathered together in times of discord, these creatures would automatically assume that the minority was to blame. This country's citizens had tarred Yulan's name before, and they seemed all too eager to brand Gia in the same way.

"The prince of Sina?" a classmate asked. "You're interested in *that* guy?"

"Well, I'm more interested in his empire," Yulan said.

"A strong thirst for knowledge is great to have, but...best not to get close."

"Ha ha, right."

Yulan gave the appropriate smile and response every time, and in doing so gave others the mistaken impression that he agreed with them. Little did they know that by coating every word they spoke about Gia with disdain, they made themselves dwindle in importance to Yulan. He never bothered to remember the names of such people, nor the contents of their conversations.

Guess he really didn't have any important info.

He had gleaned about as much as he expected from chatting with the boy in Gia's class. The isolated foreign prince hadn't let anything slip about himself, let alone about his own country. Or rather, he might have said something, but no one had paid attention.

Might be risky to get involved with him, though.

Yulan's position was more dangerously unstable than one might assume. His transformation from a child—born as an impure existence, loathed as an imitation, and tailed by the shadow of death—into a kind, gentle, and promising young man praised by all around him couldn't be explained by ordinary means. His outstandingly charming appearance and cunning intellect contributed tremendously to this change, but the major driving force was Yulan's desperation to push himself forward, to survive.

Not that anyone was seriously considering stamping out Yulan as he stood now. Without some magic method of altering the blood flowing through his veins, however, he could never shake the possibility that someone might show up to beat him back into the dirt someday.

He would have preferred to gather the information he needed without interacting with Gia...but apparently, things wouldn't be quite so easy.

I Swear I Won't Bother You AGAIN!

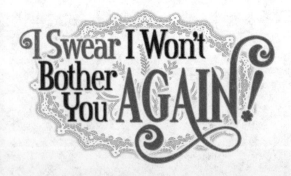

Side Story – The Foreign Prince, Part 3

INDEED, THEY WERE oddly similar even in their differences.

Unimaginable as the situation was, it came to pass in a surprisingly natural way. One might call a meeting like this inevitable or even fated, but the incredible luck involved in such chance encounters could only be appreciated after the fact.

The mountain of bread atop the table was far too much to pass for a single serving. The table seated six, although only one of those seats was occupied; Yulan didn't know if the titanic pile of bread or the person currently consuming it was to blame for the empty seats, but he would put money on the latter. The table's sole diner had tan skin, silver hair, and an all-around uncouth vibe, but his facial features in particular held a feminine delicacy. His androgynous appearance was strikingly adorable in contrast to Yulan's conventionally handsome visage.

He was Gia Forte, the Sina Empire's third prince.

Here was the subject of Yulan's curiosity, sitting directly in front of him. Hesitant as he was to get involved with the prince, this was a perfect opportunity to find out what he needed—although he wouldn't realize this until much later. At that time, the question on his mind unconsciously slipped out of his mouth.

"You're going to eat all that?"

"Huh?" Gia responded.

Yulan recognized himself in the face peering up at him. Gia's affect was flat and almost completely devoid of emotion. His expression was similarly blank. One thing was clear in an instant: Gia was utterly uninterested in other people.

Yulan had soft hair and shining, golden eyes that drooped slightly at the edges to invoke a kind, sweet aura. His facial features were the epitome of classic beauty, and that carried through to his body. He was tall, built with muscle and rich with masculine charm. Gia was the more muscular of the two, but Yulan was the one who left the impression of mighty strength upon the masses.

He was Yulan Cugurs, viewed as a gentle and kindhearted classmate to all.

Yulan's web of relationships spanned wide enough that even Gia, who rarely interacted with others, had seen him before. It spoke to the thoroughness and canny manner in which Yulan comported himself that even someone like Gia recognized him at once. Recognition was the extent of their relationship, however. Gia found little overlap between the impression he had of Yulan and the real person in front of his eyes. This boy, so eager to respond to everyone with a smile, currently stood nearby with an emotionless expression.

This was how they met, with a momentary exchange of words that couldn't even be called a conversation. Had they continued to pass each other without interacting further, this meeting would be nothing but a coincidental collision in both of their lives. Had this encounter, too, led to them becoming best friends, then it might have been fair to call it an act of fate.

❧

Gia didn't know why he was feeling nostalgic about the day they'd met. He wasn't the type to have more than a passing thought about the past, and on the rare occasions that he did, it slid out of his mind as easily as a half-remembered dream. His situation had slowly changed since the day he'd met Yulan, but that certainly wasn't due to an effort on either of their parts. The environment had been sculpted around Gia and Yulan's interactions. It could be chalked up to Yulan's popularity to a degree, but Gia felt no obligation to be especially thankful or resentful to him for it.

To Gia, this country remained boring, cramped, and troublesome. He had long since lost interest; it wasn't worth expecting change.

"You're still here?" Yulan said, stepping into their classroom.

"Welcome back, man. Done with your little chat?" Gia asked him.

"Well, you know. It wasn't drawn-out or anything."

"Ooh, so it was a confession?"

"Who knows? I gave a suitable apology and came back here." Yulan's brow was furrowed in annoyance.

Since Yulan had no perception of love, Gia wondered if the courage to confess to him should be praised or ridiculed. Regardless, one thing was clear: Yulan's outward appearance had worked wonders. Gia, who knew Yulan's true nature, wondered what the confessor saw in him and how much confidence it had taken to confess—especially since Yulan would never direct a shred of genuine friendliness toward anybody but one person. Violette Rem Vahan was the one girl whose existence meant the world to Yulan.

Aah, that's why. It dawned on him that he'd been reminiscing about their first encounter because he'd finally seen this man's treasure up close. Back then, he'd almost been deceived himself.

"That reminds me. Someone just came to see you."

"Huh?"

"The message was... 'I'm sorry for today, and I'll make it up to you later.'"

"Urk!"

Yulan immediately grabbed his bag and rushed out of the classroom without saying goodbye. Only one person registered on his radar, it seemed, given how quickly he'd discerned the origin of that message. The vexation on his face had vanished. He was in such a hurry to see her that Gia's presence had been wiped clean out of his mind.

He's one interesting fella.

Gia would never experience the feelings of love, attachment, and unconditional acceptance Yulan felt for Violette. Sacred, beautiful, filthy, or corrupted—Gia didn't know which words, if any, applied to Yulan's feelings. Nor did he care. What he found fascinating was this complete transformation in a man who was uncaring and inconsiderate to a fault. And all for the sake of a single person!

"Wonder how this is gonna turn out? Heh..."

Recalling how Yulan's expressionless mask crumbled in an instant brought a reflexive smile to Gia's lips. There were few to whom Yulan opened up to more than Gia. Even among those few, there was but a single person that he would prioritize to the detriment of all else. She was the center of his world, and to say that was neither platitude, flattery, nor some fleeting bit of fantasy. Yulan truly would offer his body, soul, and even life to the person he treasured.

Gia would never understand how Yulan had cultivated this fairy tale of his into reality, and that was why it was irresistibly interesting to him. Where did the limits of Yulan's devotion and conviction lie? What kind of decision would Yulan's beautiful treasure make in the end? And who stood to gain from whatever answers emerged from those questions?

Duralia held no pleasures for Gia. There was little here to offer him stimulation. Nothing he came across excited him. Yet he was satisfied with his life enough not to care.

Gia had found a toy worthy of his attention at last...a friend who attracted his interest.

I Swear I Won't Bother You AGAIN!

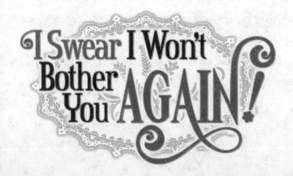

AFTERWORD

H ELLO, this is Reina Soratani.

We managed to release a second volume with the help and cooperation of many people. Thank you all very much! I hope that you derived at least a little pleasure from reading it.

I had serialized over ninety chapters before I noticed it. Even though I'm the author, I couldn't believe that it had continued for this long. I had planned for the story to conclude at around seventy chapters...but I soon realized that to expect that my writing would go exactly as planned was far beyond the realm of wishful thinking. I've been considering trying my hand at short stories this year, so I must try harder to wrangle my unruly sentences.

Recently, I've been working while enjoying some chocolate and listening to the *Let's Be Novelists* radio show. One day, I realized that I was so absorbed in the radio program that my hands had stopped moving. I was laughing, and the number of sentences was at a complete standstill... I decided it made far more sense to indulge myself *after* work instead. It also brought to my attention that I'd been eating too much chocolate.

This time, the main storyline focused on the exam arc. I enjoyed my own school exams, since they meant I could return home earlier and spend more time playing, but I imagine that Vio hated them for those same reasons. Envisioning it made my desire to kill Vio's dad skyrocket. Sadly, the high school textbook I received from my big sister wasn't as helpful as I portrayed here... though that was probably because of my disdain for studying. I hope that I'll find a use for it one day.

I had a lot of fun whenever Claudia appeared—I can write Yulan in a really vulgar way in those scenes. Forgive me, Your Highness! I enjoy the conversations between Yulan and Vio, but I do have to consider how Yulan never breaks character in front of her. I also love the cute, drawling way he talks whenever she's around. Considering my penchant for scenes where Marin drops her polite speech and curses, I might have an inclination toward speech gimmicks like those.

In terms of who's easiest to write—tone and personality included—Gia is top of my list. His casual way of speaking is really similar to mine, so his lines are a breeze to come up with. There's no need for etiquette, flattery, or sugarcoating, so the words come right to me even when he has to say things that are difficult to express. I'm a huge fan of Gia to begin with, to be fair. Especially his looks.

Speaking of which, the star of the second volume's side story is none other than Gia! I was desperate to write the story of how he and Yulan crossed paths, but I didn't know where it would fit into the main story. I took advantage of the bonus story to bring it to light. I hope that I faithfully depicted Gia's inner life—or rather, the parts of him besides his tendency to get bored and act as a spectator. Ultimately, I feel that he came across as having a rather bad personality, but that feels in the spirit of what I aimed to write. Gia doesn't have an innately good personality, but he does affect one in whatever he does. That's what I wanted to express.

Another point of interest: whenever Yulan is with Gia, he acts differently from usual, which makes him very fun to write. Yulan is fundamentally cool and tends to look down on others, but things never go the way he wants around Gia, so it ticks him off. Gia is freed from all sorts of restraints, so Yulan thinks that it would be foolish to try to assert dominance over him. In that sense, Gia might be the strongest character in the cast. Apathy is pretty powerful.

Gia's apathy has its downsides, too, in that it's hard to depict his inner thoughts. Easy as it was to write his lines, he still eluded me. What did he find the most fun? The most painful? And what was Yulan to Gia? Trying to comprehend what Gia might think about when he was alone with his thoughts drove me to the brink of madness.

This goes for all the characters, but how come my own creations move in ways I didn't expect? Oh, how many times I had thought they would follow the plot's progression! But it never happens!

There were many more stories that refused to fit tidily into the main plot, while some stories read more like parodies. I dithered over whether I should write them down and cram them into the web novel on *Let's Be Novelists*. The more depressing the main story became, the more I wanted to write something uplifting... It's the same urge as craving something sour after eating something sweet.

In the Volume 1 afterword, I mentioned Marin's and Yulan's "Violette Convention." I would like to cordially invite Rosette there as a new participant. Unfortunately, there are far too few openings in the main story for any stories about this convention where they express their love for Violette.

Is the main story approaching a happy ending or leaving it far in the distance? Are Vio's current feelings leading her closer to happiness or resignation? People may be capable of transforming their love into strength, but by the same token, some can transmute that love into bitter contempt. Vio's mom was fully capable of sacrificing others for her own needs, but what about Vio? And if it did come to that, who would pay the price for her? Even I don't know.

I wish to express my heartfelt gratitude to everyone who has been so kind as to be involved with this book. I am truly delighted that a second volume has taken form. To those in charge who contacted me late at night and accompanied me when I was slow with my work; to the incredible Haru Harukawa who, together with the manga adaptation, brought the world of this story to life with amazing art; to everyone in the editorial department; to the readers who picked up this book. Thank you all so very much!

The manga adaptation has already been published, so to those who haven't read it yet: I implore you to please give it a read. Just like with Volume 1, I have written a short story there as well!

Imperfect as I remain, I would deeply appreciate your continued support in the future. I hope we can see each other again!

January 2020